The Ghost Hunter at Chillwood Castle

Ivan Jones

To my old friend, Tony Bolderston

Scholastic Children's Books,
Commonwealth House, 1-19 New Oxford Street,
London WC1A 1NU, UK
a division of Scholastic Ltd
London ~ New York ~ Toronto ~ Sydney ~ Auckland
Mexico City ~ New Delhi ~ Hong Kong

First published in the UK by Scholastic Ltd, 2000

Copyright © Ivan Jones, 2000

ISBN 0 439 01404 2

Typeset by
Cambrian Typesetters, Frimley, Camberley, Surrey
Printed by
Cox and Wyman Ltd, Reading, Berks

10 9 8 7 6 5 4 3 2

Chapter 1

Dead or Alive!

Roddy saw a dark, narrow staircase in front of him.

He didn't hesitate.

His feet hit the worn stone steps and began pounding up them, faster and faster.

He knew the Ghost Hunter was behind, closing in on him. He heard her shriek: *"Dead or alive! I want him dead or alive!"*

"No," he whispered. "No!"

His legs began to ache. He stumbled on a crumbling, rotten step. Part of the stone broke away underfoot. He snatched at the sharp rock of the wall, grazing his fingers. Then he staggered on as the staircase wound tighter and tighter.

At last he reached the top and flung himself out

into the cold, glittering night air. He was choking for breath.

"*Ghost Saver!*"

The words whirled up the stone stairs behind him and swished round his ears.

"*Disgusting Ghost Saver!*"

He took a step across the rotting parapet. Then he glanced back over his shoulder.

He saw a tall figure in a billowing black cape; a figure with piercing beady eyes and a long nose who swooped towards him like a ferocious vulture. Roddy gaped over the parapet in front of him. There was a terrible, yawning drop.

Roddy froze on the spot. He felt two claw-like hands grip his shoulders.

"*Got you! Got you at last!*" screamed the icy voice.

"No!" Roddy screamed. "No! Never! Never!"

"Wake up, Roddy!" William Povey hissed. "Wake up!"

Roddy Oliver sat up and stared round him.

"It's me, mate! What 'appened? You wus kickin' and makin' a real old row, you was."

"You're not Mrs Croker," Roddy shouted. "You're not ... are you?"

"Course I ain't! I'm your ghost-friend, William Povey! Remember? Do I look like an 'orrible old battle-axe?"

Roddy shook his head. He was very pale. His fair hair was pasted to his forehead.

"But it was so real!" Roddy said. "The Ghost Hunter – Mrs Croker – was chasing me up these steps and one of the steps broke under my foot."

"It's your big clod-hoppers, mate! Break anything them fings would! Listen, she ain't gonna hurt you, now. The police have got her in custody, ain't they? Until her trial. For kidnapping Mrs Humphries. You remember? She won't be doing no more ghost-hunting for a while, will she? 'Specially if they send her to clink, where she ought to be sent. Right?"

Roddy gave William a weak smile and got out of bed. His legs still felt wobbly. But at least he felt safe now.

"I suppose I must be worried. In case she tries to catch you again," Roddy said. "I keep remembering her coming to our house and spraying Ghost Immobilizing Vapour everywhere and trying to bottle you."

"Yeah," William said. "I suppose she got pretty close, didn't she?"

"It's giving me nightmares. In case she escapes and comes after you again!"

"She won't!" William said. "You, me and Tessa beat her, didn't we, me old mate? We beat her good and proper. She's done for now. Well and truly!"

"What time is it?" Roddy said.

"Midnight. *Ghosting time!*" William laughed. "Ain't that what we agreed?"

Roddy nodded. But he was still shocked by his dream.

At that moment, the church clock began to chime twelve. As it stopped, William heard another noise.

"What was that?" he said.

"What?" Roddy said. He listened intently.

"It's out there," William whispered. "On the landing!"

It was something or someone moaning.

Then the bedroom door handle moved gently down.

Click!

The door opened a crack. And through the gap crawled a huge black, hairy spider with legs as long as knitting needles.

Roddy gasped. Little shivers of fear ran down his

spine. He took a couple of steps back. And as he did so he tripped over and fell on to his bed.

Instantly, the spider flew across the room, its eight legs waggling in the air. And landed right on Roddy's face.

Roddy screamed...

But a hand clamped over his mouth, stifling his cry.

"Shh," his sister, Tessa, said. She plucked the spider from his face. "It's only a toy!"

"You ape!" Roddy yelled, as he struggled off the bed. "That was a really stupid trick, Tessa! I could have died of fright!"

William was laughing. "Nar, it was quite a good 'un, mate," he said. He picked up the fake spider and shook it in mid-air just in front of Tessa's face.

"Pack it in, William!" Tessa shrieked. "It's not fair! You know I can't see you!"

"You should be like yer brother," William laughed. "Get yourself some second sight! Eh, Roddy?"

"Yeah," Roddy said. "Go on, William, scare *her* now!"

William held the spider and floated with it round the room, swooping it down over Tessa's hair. This made Tessa cross. She liked to be the boss, because she was the oldest, but the boys often stopped her.

"Give me a shoe-brush so that I can see you!" Tessa demanded.

"Don't!" Roddy shouted. "It serves you right!"

William dangled the spider in front of her eyes again.

She quickly swiped it to the floor. "William," she shouted. "Don't be so obnoxious!"

"Ob – what?" William said.

"She's swallowed the dictionary again!" Roddy said. "That's all she can find to eat, isn't it, Tessa? She's already eaten the Oxford and the Collins. Eh, Tess, your name should be Tess-aurus!"

"Yours should be Rod-ent!" Tessa snapped. "Rodent Roddy!"

"Come on, you two," William said. "No more of this scrapping. You said you wanted a midnight fly!"

He took two shoe-brushes from his pockets and handed them to Roddy and Tessa. Immediately they felt a cold, silvery tingle run along their arms and spread through their bodies. Almost at once they became invisible and ghostly.

Tessa smiled at William. She could see him clearly now. He was wearing the cap which was too large for him, jammed over his eyes. Stuffed into the pockets of his grimy, long coat were dusters and polish. William's broken and blackened teeth gave his face a cheeky grin.

"Ready then?" he said.

"Mum and Dad won't be back from their party for another hour at least," Roddy said.

"Open that window," Tessa cried.

"No need!" Roddy said.

"Oh, I forgot," Tessa said, as she swept back her long red hair.

"Keep hold of that brush!" William said.

"I *will*! I'm not quite stupid, you know!" Tessa snapped.

"Not *quite*?" Roddy said.

Tessa felt a jangle of excitement, as she thought herself upwards, floating directly above Roddy's bed. Then, with a little flick of her feet, she flew towards the glass in the window. When her outstretched fingers reached it, there was no resistance. The pane simply gave a tiny ripple and then she was through it – outside in the crisp darkness. Roddy and William followed.

"Look at those stars!" Roddy called. He did a loop round the chimney pots.

All three of them swooped down, close to the ground. Then up into the sky.

"I'm a swallow!" Tessa squealed. "I can skim over the tree-tops!"

"Take it steady," William said. "Don't want no accidents."

"Stop nagging, William!" Tessa tutted. "I'm the oldest here!"

"Oh no, you're not!" William chuckled. "I'm about a hundred and ten, I am! When I was born, *Queen Victoria* was on the throne! I've been wandering around and about ever since! I seen loads of fings I have. Loads!"

Roddy sat on the ridge of the Olivers' roof and looked up at the beautiful, starry sky. It was like black velvet pierced with silver flowers.

"I can see the Plough and the Seven Sisters," he said.

"*Seven* sisters?" William said. "Ain't one enough?"

"More than enough!" Roddy laughed. "One is one too many!" He flew into the sky getting higher and higher.

"If you get to the moon, stay there!" Tessa shouted.

Roddy turned and rocketed back.

"Let's take a look at the churchyard! See what it's like at midnight!" he yelled over his shoulder.

Away from the ugly yellow glow of street lights, the churchyard was quite dark. It was made darker by the spreading branches of yew trees. William settled on a tombstone.

Tessa landed next to him,

"It's spooky!" she whispered.

"Nice!" William replied. "Nice and *ghostly*! Like home to me, this is."

"You don't think there are any vampires around here, do you?" Roddy whispered as he peered at the fallen gravestones and strange twisted shadows.

"Ssh!" Tessa hissed. "There's something moving over there!" She pointed across the graveyard.

Roddy bit his lip. He stared into the gloom. His eyes were almost popping out. The hairs stood up on the back of his neck.

William turned slowly, searching the broken and fallen tombstones.

Suddenly the children heard groaning.

"Look!" Tessa said.

An ugly, hairy hand, with nails like black hooks,

appeared at the top of a gravestone. The children could hear the nails scrape against the granite.

Roddy gasped.

Then an old man stood up from behind the stone. He wore a huge, ragged overcoat, tied up with string. His hair was completely white and hung round his head like a mane. He kept swigging from a bottle.

"Oh, it's only a tramp," William whispered. "He's 'ad a drop too much by the look of him."

The man began to sing, "Give me the moonlight, give me the stars..." As he sang, he swayed about.

He began to stagger towards the children.

"He can't see us," William said. "He finks he's all on his own, he does!"

"I don't like it!" Tessa said. "Let's get away!"

"Where?" Roddy said.

Tessa looked at the church tower. "Up there!" she said.

"Right to the top?" Roddy said.

"Yes. The higher the better!"

The three children flew up and landed on a steep sloping roof. "That's safer," Tessa said. "The highest place in the village!"

They stared back down at the tramp as he

danced about a long way below them. He was still singing.

Then Tessa heard a creaking above her. A copper weather vane pivoted gently in the wind, at the top-most pinnacle of the roof. It was in the shape of a cockerel sitting on top of an arrow. Tessa floated up to it. She reached out to touch it.

Without thinking, she let the shoe-brush she was holding slip from her fingers. It hit the lead covering of the roof, bounced, and Roddy caught it.

"Tess!" he yelled.

But without the brush, Tessa couldn't fly. Her full weight thumped heavily on to the lead roof.

"Help!" she screamed.

She made a terrified grab at the weather vane and missed. As she slid, she snatched at the lead, tearing her nails. Frantically trying to get a grip somewhere, she scorched her knees, bruised her elbows, scraped her cheek. She stuck out her boots to slow herself down. The soles squealed like a pair of worn-out brakes. But she didn't stop. She slid as if she was greased in butter. She slewed from the top of the lead roof to the bottom. The next moment, she crashed over the edge and plunged sickeningly towards the flagstones far below.

Chapter 2

Falling – Falling!

The tramp was still singing near the bottom of the church tower.

He heard Tessa scream. He looked up and his mouth fell open like a small black hole. He clapped his hand over it, as he saw a girl in jeans and a white jacket tumble off the roof, way above him.

Past the top buttress, she fell. Past the gargoyles, past the clock, past the stained-glass window. She fell so fast that all the tramp could see was a blur. He watched, rooted to the spot. He tried to cry out, but his voice was stuck in his throat. He tried to think, but his mind was numb with drink. She whizzed down, down, down, faster and faster. Soon, he knew, it would be too late.

"No..." he muttered. "No ... no..."

He had never seen anything like it and his whole body shook with fear. Tessa plummeted like a stone. The tramp closed his eyes in terror. Then opened them again.

And that was when Tessa stopped. Right in front of him. Right in front of his purple face and swollen cheeks. A couple of metres from the ground. He goggled at her for a fraction of a second. His knees buckled under him as if he was going to faint.

And then she vanished.

The tramp stared. He gawped all round the church yard. He glowered up at the tower. No sign of anybody. Nobody falling. No squelched body on the floor. Nothing! His eyes grew big like a couple of hard-boiled eggs. They swung from left to right. Then he looked down at the bottle in his hand. He was no longer drunk.

"The drink! Tch, tch!" he muttered. "The stinking, rotten drink!"

He hurled the bottle as far away as he could and dashed from the church yard, yelling as if he was mad.

"Forget something?" William said to Tessa.

Tessa threw her arms round William's neck and started to cry.

By some stupendous effort, by some incredible ghostly power, William had thrown himself off the roof, overtaken Tessa and grabbed her hand!

"Sorry..." she sobbed. "How could I?"

"Blimey, girl, don't mention it."

William gently put her on to a lower roof. It was much flatter than the one she'd fallen off. Roddy flew down next to her.

"Take some deep breaths," he said. She was trembling violently. Roddy turned to William.

"Thank you, William. You saved her life."

"It was nuffink," William said. "Nuffink."

"How could I be so ... so ... *stupid*?" Tessa whispered.

Roddy put his arm round her. "Easily..." he said, with a giggle. Tessa gave a little choking laugh, her eyes still full of tears.

"Anyone can make a mistake, can't they?" William said. "Specially when they're tired."

Tessa rubbed her head.

"What's the matter?" Roddy said.

"I must have banged my head on the roof when I fell," Tessa said. "It hurts a bit."

She shivered and then looked around her as if coming back out of a dream. The boys watched her. Tessa's eyes were suddenly very bright, staring.

"William!" she gasped.

Roddy didn't understand. "What? Tessa? What about William?"

Tessa smiled now, sweeping away her tears. She looked carefully at Roddy's anxious face, then back at William.

"What is it, Tess?" Roddy said softly.

"I can *SEE WILLIAM*! Without holding a brush! I can *SEE* him!" she shrieked.

"You got second sight an' all. Just like your brother," William said. "That bang on the head has woken it up!"

"Wait a minute," Roddy said. "Look away, Tess."

Tessa did so.

"Now look back again," Roddy said. "Can you still see him?"

"Yes. Quite clearly," Tessa cried.

"Fantastic!" William shouted. "We won't have to keep no secrets from you no more, will we? That's the way it should be with us three! Come on, Tess. We'll have to get back. You gotta fly before you lose your nerve."

15

"OK," she whispered. "I'm ready." But she was still shaking like a leaf as she took the brush from William.

William held Tessa's free hand as they rose again into the air and slowly flew towards the Olivers' house. It was nearly one o'clock.

As they passed over the silent streets, they saw a car with a pair of bright headlamps swing in to their drive.

"That's Mum and Dad!" Roddy yelled. "They're early!"

"We'd better get in quick, before they notice we're missing!" Tessa said.

Mr and Mrs Oliver got out of the car.

"Lovely night!" Mrs Oliver said, looking up at the stars.

"It's all right," William said. "They can't see us. We're three ghosts, remember?"

"Yuk!" Roddy said. "They're kissing on the doorstep!"

"Hurry up!" Tessa cried. "They'll be inside in a minute!"

The front door closed. The children darted for Roddy's bedroom window and were about to go inside when an old van roared along the road and pulled up in the street outside the Olivers' house. Its lights went off.

"Who's that?" William said.

"Don't know," Tessa said. The van door creaked open. A thin, gangly youth dressed in a long shabby coat almost fell out of it.

"Sniff … sniff … sniff." The young man wiped his nose along his sleeve and glanced up over his shoulder at the Olivers' house. Then from the rear of the van he took a parcel.

"What's he up to?" Roddy said.

"Sniff … sniff … sniff." As he moved, he held his left shoulder higher than the right. And as he walked his body rolled as if he was on board ship. He held his head at an angle, as if he was constantly looking sideways.

"He's coming to our house!" Roddy said.

"Delivering parcels in the middle of the night?" Tessa said.

"Must think he's Father Christmas!" Roddy said.

The youth placed the parcel carefully on the doorstep. He sniffed again. Then he hurried back to his van. He spat out of its window and drove away.

"Ugh!" Tessa said. "How revolting!"

"Let's go and investigate," Roddy said. But William was pointing through a gap in the curtains of Roddy's bedroom.

"Your mum's already in your room! Quick! Follow me." He flew straight through the wall and right under Mrs Oliver's nose.

"Roddy? Roddy?" Mrs Oliver was saying. "Where are you?"

"Come on," William hissed. "In the bathroom. You can call her from there."

"See you in the morning," Tessa said, as she drifted through the wall into her own bedroom.

"Roddy!" Mrs Oliver called. Her voice sounded a bit scared.

"In here, Mum," Roddy mumbled, trying to sound sleepy. "In the toilet."

"Oh ... oh, you're all right?" she said. "I thought you'd be fast asleep now."

"Yeah, I'm OK," Roddy said. "Goodnight."

"Goodnight," his mum said.

When the coast was clear, Roddy went to his bedroom.

"Phew, that was close," he said.

William had shrunk himself and was lying down in a box of tissues.

"Not half," William said. "Who do you think that geezer was?"

"I think I've seen him before," Roddy replied. "Delivering things to the village shop. Why he should be bringing something out at this time of night, I don't know!"

William yawned.

"I'm so tired, mate."

"Yeah," Roddy said. "I reckon I'll nod off as soon as my head touches the pillow."

There was no reply from William. He was already fast asleep.

Chapter 3

A Shock for Mr Oliver

The next morning, Tessa floated through the wall into Roddy's room. She still had one of William's brushes in her hand.

"Roddy! William!" she shouted. "Wake up!" She threw a pillow at Roddy.

"Stop it!" Roddy groaned. "I need my beauty sleep!"

"Yeah," Tessa said. "Lots of it!"

"Cor blimey!" William chirped up. "What time is it? I was dreamin' about a geezer who used to come to my shoe-shine stall. Bloke called Belcher Smiff."

"We'd better get downstairs right away if you want to find out what's in that parcel," Tessa shouted. "I just heard Dad bringing it in!"

Roddy jumped out of bed. He threw on some clothes.

William quickly shot to his proper size. He held out a shoe-brush to Roddy.

"Let's give 'im a little surprise, shall we, mates?"

Mr Oliver had the parcel in front of him on the dining-room table. He was scratching his head and bits of dandruff were falling on to the carpet.

"Roddy and Tessa Oliver," Mr Oliver muttered as he read the label. He picked up the parcel and turned it round and round.

"He's a right old Nosey Parker, your old man, ain't he?" William said.

"Yes, he is!" Tessa said crossly. They had floated into the room through the ceiling and were hovering just over Mr Oliver's head. Mr Oliver tore off a little strip of brown paper from the parcel.

"Obviously not a box from a store," he said. "Much too battered. You have to be so careful with children these days." Mr Oliver sighed to himself. "You never know what they're sending off for."

"What a cheek!" Tessa fumed. "Let's materialize right behind him. I'd like to give him a piece of my mind!"

But Mr Oliver suddenly leapt forwards and began to rip off all the paper from the box.

"I really think I ought to investigate," he said. "A good father ought to check these things!"

"Holy horrors!" Tessa shrieked. She gave her shoe-brush to William and immediately became visible right behind her father. Mr Oliver was just removing the last wrapping from the box. He was very excited.

"DAD!" she shrieked.

Mr Oliver nearly jumped out of his skin. It made him straighten up smartly, pulling open the box as he did so.

Immediately, there was a loud BANG! Bits of brown paper shot up and scattered everywhere. There was a sharp hissing sound from the box. The room began filling with a fine mist.

"William!" Roddy shouted in terror. "Get away. It's *Ghost Immobilizing Vapour*! I'm sure of it!"

"Give us that brush," said William, snatching it from Roddy's hand. "If any of it touches you while you've got it, you're a goner an' all!"

A second BANG sent even more vapour exploding in all directions. Mr Oliver was stunned.

He stood, removing strips of paper from his face, soaked to the skin. So was Tessa.

"What the dickens is going on?" Mr Oliver yelled. Drops of vapour dripped from the end of his nose. He glared angrily at Tessa and Roddy. "Is this your idea of a stupid joke?"

"It wasn't us, was it, Tessa?" Roddy said.

"No," Tessa replied.

Mr Oliver was white as a sheet. Droplets of vapour clung to his hair, his eyebrows, his ears.

"Whatever will you think of next?" he shrieked.

"But, Dad!" Tessa tried to explain. "The parcel was addressed to us, wasn't it?"

"Don't you try to talk your way out of it!"

"You shouldn't have opened it!" Tessa shouted.

"Go and fetch a mop and cloth and clean up this mess. Now!" roared her father.

Roddy ducked under the table. "William?" he called. "William? Where are you?"

Mr Oliver stared at his son in amazement. "What's got into you?" he growled "Have you gone completely bonkers?" He strode to the door and opened it.

"Go!" he said.

Roddy and Tessa sidled out of the room to the kitchen.

When they returned, Mr Oliver was still standing in the same place. He was fuming.

"I'm going to be late for work because of your idiotic pranks! Get it all cleared away!" he shouted. He barged out of the door and went to tidy himself up.

"William," Roddy whispered. "William!"

Tessa looked behind the curtains and in one of the cupboards.

Nothing.

"D'you think it got him?" she said anxiously.

"I don't know," Roddy said.

"Oh, I hope he isn't stuck somewhere … *immobilized*," Tessa said. "In the wall cavity, or something. You know?"

At that moment, a pile of soot fell from the chimney and dropped heavily into the fireplace.

"Ugh!" Roddy spluttered. "What next?"

A cloud of black dust drifted from the grate up into the room. Tessa coughed.

"That was 'orrible!" a voice muttered.

"William?" Roddy whispered. "Is that you?"

"All right, me old mates?" the dust cloud said. "It's me, all right. Blimey. Been stuck up that chimbley I have. Look at the state of me!"

Roddy laughed. "William! What are you doing? Floating round in that load of soot!"

"Only place I could fink of!" William said. He dropped down to the carpet and stood facing them, his crooked smile showing through his darkened face.

"Still, I escaped that vapour, didn't I? Thank heavens. Only fing is, I'm worried now. Who's that geezer what brought it here? That's what I wants to know!"

"Me, too," Roddy said. "Look, this canister's got the remains of a label. You can just read ... *obilizing vap*..."

"D'you think that delivery man knew what was in it?" Tessa said. "Or did somebody put him up to it?"

"I don't know," Roddy replied.

"Dad's coming back!" Tessa snapped.

William handed them a brush each. "Let's scarper!"

"Dad won't be pleased with this lot," Tessa said, pointing at the soot all over the place.

But as the door opened, the three children shot quickly through the ceiling.

Mrs Oliver came off the telephone.

"That was another call about strange goings-on last night," she said to Mr Oliver. "It's going to make a great article for the paper. I've already started writing it, but with all this new information coming in, I'm going to make it longer – with lots of anecdotal stuff in it. You know, personal accounts of what has been happening to people."

"What's going on?" Mr Oliver replied as he hurried around collecting his tools together for work.

"I don't know," Mrs Oliver said. "But that was Jim Hatfield on the phone and he said that around midnight last night, all the clocks in his house stopped ticking and got stuck at exactly the same time."

"Huh," Mr Oliver said. "Clocks do stop. Coincidence, I'd guess."

"Seven clocks? I don't think so," Mrs Oliver said. "And what's more, every time he turned the TV *off*, it turned itself back on again!"

"Well, that is a bit odd," Mr Oliver said. "Do

exploding parcels full of lemonade spray count as extra-terrestrial?" he muttered. "And soot falling down the chimney and making a dreadful mess everywhere?"

"No. And we're talking about the paranormal, dear. Not extra-terrestrial."

"It's all the same if you ask me – *bunkum*!" Mr Oliver said. "See you later. I'm doing a door at the shop."

"Right, love, see you later. Oh, by the way, did you hear the news?"

"What news?"

"The radio news. That Mrs Croker has escaped from custody."

Mr Oliver came back into the room. "What? Done a runner?"

"Yes. They were taking her to court. One minute she was in the prison van, the next she was out!"

"Well, if she's escaped, she'll probably head abroad. I don't suppose we'll ever see her again!"

"I certainly hope not," Mrs Oliver said. "She was like a maniac, spraying all over our house with that air-freshener."

Roddy heard the last sentence as he came into the room. "You talking about Mrs Croker?"

"Yes, Roddy," his mum said. "She's escaped on her way to court."

"She *can't* have!" Roddy cried.

"I'm afraid she has."

"Don't worry, son," his dad said. "She won't come back here in a hurry."

Roddy's head was whirling. There was a question he'd come down to ask his parents. What was it?

"Oh, yes – who was that delivery bloke—"

"Man, dear. Not bloke."

"That delivery man, who kept coming to the shop when Mrs Croker was there?"

Mr Oliver scratched his head. "I remember him. Funny name. A bit of a weirdo as well."

"De-Sniff wasn't it? A French name, perhaps?" Mrs Oliver said.

"That's right, Jan," Mr Oliver said. "De-Sniff. Suited him as well!"

Chapter 4

Hide-out

"I am not living in a revolting caravan!" Mrs Croker strode ahead of De-Sniff. Her cloak swept out behind her and flicked in his face.

"No ... no, guv'nor. The caravan's for me. I just stumbled on it in Burnham's Wood. What I got for you is near to it!"

Mrs Croker crashed through the undergrowth which overhung the old railway line she and De-Sniff were trying to follow.

"It'd better be good."

De-Sniff blew his knobbly, blistered nose between his fingers and gasped. "Oh, it is, boss. Really, really good. It's a place nobody'll ever find. Not in a million years. You'll be safe from them police an' all!"

He ran a few paces, stumbling to keep up with her, but it was no use, he always seemed to fall back behind her tall, striding figure.

"You know there's a big event coming up, don't you? And everything must be in place. Everything! D'you hear me?" she snapped.

"Yes, boss."

"I need to gather things – materials, details. I need to make preparations!"

"Yes, boss."

Their footsteps cracked on broken twigs, their arms pushed back twisted branches.

"How much further?" Mrs Croker hissed. Her sharp eyes narrowed like poisoned darts. Her restless sharp face moved ceaselessly.

"Just a bit more. Up there."

"Where?"

"Away from the line ... down that gulley."

Mrs Croker snarled through a pair of pale, snake-thin lips. "Good! Quite acceptable."

"Yeah. I done a good job, ain't I, boss? You'll like it."

"I'd better, De-Sniff! I'd better!"

De-Sniff trembled slightly, but then became enthusiastic again. "I'm learning, ain't I, guv?"

The narrow, overgrown gulley led to a patch of

spindly, seedling trees. They gave the land an air of decay and loss.

"Over there, chief." De-Sniff pointed at an arched shape beyond some thick bracken.

Mrs Croker spied a decrepit caravan. It had once been cream and green. Now it was filthy. Slime and fungus grew all over it and out of it.

"S'mine," De-Sniff smiled. "All me own."

"Huh!" Mrs Croker said. Then she glared at him. "Well? Where is it?"

"Oh, yeah, right." De-Sniff gave a sly cackle and went past his caravan, across a clearing.

He led Mrs Croker to a cutting in the ground. There were some concrete steps leading down. They descended until they came to a low-set door. De-Sniff opened the door and went inside. Mrs Croker followed.

"I got some lights," De-Sniff said proudly.

Mrs Croker stopped still. She stood examining the place, her huge long nose twitching.

"It's caves!" De-Sniff said excitedly. He licked his lips and sniffed hard. He looked up, sideways at Mrs Croker.

"This way, boss."

He felt the wall of the cave with his hand and made his way in the semi-darkness until he came to another larger door. He opened it and went into an inner room — a larger inner cave.

Mrs Croker stared round it. De-Sniff waited, hopefully, like a dog waiting for crumbs.

"Secret, ain't it, boss?" he whispered.

"Perfect!" Mrs Croker snapped.

De-Sniff almost leaped into the air.

"I thought you'd like it. I did. I thought: it's just right for you, boss."

"Shut up!"

"Yes, boss."

"You know what we want, don't you?"

"I can bring things in the van. There's a narrow track which nobody uses. It's near."

"Ghosts, De-Sniff," Mrs Croker hissed suddenly. Her eyes glazed over. "Rows and rows of them. I'll bottle the beastly fiends!" She shuddered. "I won't *rest* until I've bottled them. The whole danged, blasted lot of them! D'you hear me, De-Sniff? Do you hear me?"

Mrs Croker's voice had risen to a terrifying frenzy. Suddenly she turned on him. Her eyes went white with hatred.

De-Sniff shuddered as if he'd just been dropped into a bath of ice.

Chapter 5

Ghost in the Classroom

On their way to school, William's eyes kept popping out of his head. And his ears waggled up and down as though they weren't connected to him.

"What's up?" Roddy said.

"Nervous, mate."

"Because of the Ghost Hunter?" Roddy said.

"Yeah," William shivered.

"Me, too," Roddy said.

"She's on my trail again!" William said. "I *know* she is! And that geezer, De-Sniff or whatever his name is, bringing that parcel of GIV – he *could* be her helper."

The boys went through the school gates and into the building.

In the main school corridor, Wally Crabbe crept up behind Roddy and tried to trip him up.

"Hey, pack it in!" Roddy said, turning round to face Wally – a flabby boy with a face like a sponge cake.

"I didn't do anything," Wally smirked. "You must have tripped over your own daft feet."

"Oh yeah?" Roddy snapped.

"Yeah. Wanna make somethin' of it?"

Before Roddy could reply, Old Nosey, the school caretaker, came marching up, his huge bulbous conk leading the way.

"Oi, you. What's your name!" he yelled at Roddy.

"It's Oliver, Uncle Jake," Wally said to the caretaker. "He's always dropping litter."

"Yeah, I thought I knew you, you 'orrible little dirt-squirt." Old Nosey strode right up to him and wagged his finger in Roddy's face. "You been droppin' litter again, ain't you?"

"No," Roddy said.

Old Nosey pointed at a heap of crisp packets and old drink cans half hidden behind some lockers.

"That wasn't me!" Roddy protested.

"Clear it up!" the caretaker said. He shoved a

black plastic dustbin bag into Roddy's hand. "Now!" He turned on his heel and wandered back to his little room to smoke one of his evil-smelling cigars.

Wally Crabbe laughed, as Roddy picked up the litter and put it into the plastic bag.

"Get lost, Wally!" Roddy muttered.

"Eh? What did you say?" Wally cried, grabbing Roddy by his coat.

He gave Roddy a shove which sent him sprawling over the plastic sack.

Roddy stood up. Wally came at him again. This time with his fists.

"'Ere, mate," William said. "Take this." He pushed a brush into Roddy's hand, just as Wally Crabbe let fly with a punch.

But Wally's fist stopped in mid-air.

Roddy had vanished.

"Eh?" Wally said. He blinked. "Behind you," Roddy said.

Wally turned. Before he could do another thing, Roddy pushed Wally backwards and he fell over the plastic bag. But he scrambled to his feet and came at Roddy in a raging temper.

"'Ere," William said, again, as he handed the brush back to Roddy.

Roddy vanished again. He and William ran to the science-lab door as the bell rang. Roddy materialized just outside the door and then went into the room. A few moments later, Wally Crabbe came in. He was glowing with anger. He couldn't believe his eyes when he saw Roddy sitting down, waiting for class to start.

"Come along, Wally," Mrs Justin said. "You're late!"

Wally flounced into a chair.

"I'm gonna pulverize you, Oliver!" he muttered under his breath. "I'm gonna break every bone in your scrawny body! I'm gonna put you through a mangle and then sieve you through a sieve!"

Mrs Justin began to take the register.

"Eh, up," William said. "Old Nosey's coming in. Jus' look at him. He don't look very happy, does he?"

The caretaker went up to Mrs Justin and began talking quickly to her. He gestured around the room.

"What's he up to now?" Roddy whispered. "Look at Mrs Justin. She looks all nervous."

"You're right there, mate. Our Mr 'Ardin' ain't one for friendly chats, is he?"

They could hear snatches of what they said.

"This room, Mrs Justin ... never tidy ... clean it up all the..."

"But *I'm* not the cleaner!" Mrs Justin protested.

"No. You ain't even..." but Old Nosey's angry words didn't reach the children.

Eventually, Old Nosey left the room and the children all settled down. Mrs Justin looked pale.

"Good morning everybody," she said. "Today we must continue with our work on formulae."

Everybody groaned. Wally Crabbe groaned loudest.

But Mrs Justin ignored them and began to write on the blackboard. As she did so, she said aloud, "Now, if $x = 1$ and $y = 3$, you can work out the whole equation easily. Very useful in experiments."

William's eyes bulged and came out of his head and floated about on strings in front of him.

"What's she on about? What's x? Does it mean extra? And y? What does that mean? Why what?"

"It's an equation!" Roddy whispered. "Ssh. I'm trying to think."

"Fink!" William said. "How can you fink when she keeps saying x this and y that? Blimey, it makes your 'ead 'urt!"

"Be thankful you don't have to do it," Roddy hissed.

William shrank himself and curled up in Roddy's pencil-case.

Towards the end of the lesson, Mrs Justin asked Wally Crabbe a question.

"What's the answer, Wally?" Mrs Justin said. "Haven't you been listening to anything I've said?"

"Yeah, I have," cried Wally, "but I can't think straight with that cupboard moving about."

"What d'you mean?" Mrs Justin said. She knew Wally Crabbe and his little tricks well enough.

"That cupboard at the back of the room, Miss. It just sort of shook itself."

William woke up. "What's he on about?"

"He said the cupboard moved."

The whole class, as well as Mrs Justin, looked at the large wooden cupboard, overladen with books and papers.

"Don't be silly, Wally," Mrs Justin said. "Just answer my question, please."

"Look, Miss!" Wally yelled. All the children turned round. To their amazement the big cupboard began to shake. Some of the papers fell from its shelves.

"It's spooked, Miss!" Wally Crabbe shrieked. He stood up. "It's spooked!"

"Don't be ridiculous," Mrs Justin said, as the other children became alarmed. "Sit down!"

Wally Crabbe sat down heavily. He scowled.

Mrs Justin walked gingerly towards the tall cupboard.

Just as she reached it, the cupboard gave another rumble. More papers tumbled to the classroom floor.

"Oh!" Mrs Justin squeaked, jumping back. Several children stood up and quickly moved away from the cupboard towards the front of the classroom.

"It ... it could be an earth tremor," Mrs Justin said. "There've been some round here lately."

"It's spooked!" Wally Crabbe yelled. He tore out of his desk and dashed towards the door.

"Wally!" Mrs Justin yelled.

But at that minute the bell rang and the whole class, apart from Roddy, rushed out of the room. Mrs Justin tried to leave in a more dignified manner. When she reached the door, however, she took one last nervous look at the cupboard and then put down her head and galloped away.

"She even forgot our homework!" Roddy said.

"Yeah?" William said. "It was a bit odd, though, weren't it? That cupboard shaking like that?"

"Yes," Roddy said. "I didn't feel any earth tremor!"

"But then," William added, "when you look at it, blimey, I mean, it's so full of all them books and papers, it's a wonder it ain't bombed to the floor years ago, ain't it?"

"What d'you think is going on in the science lab, then?" Tessa said.

They were sitting in Roddy's bedroom that evening.

"I dunno," William said. "That cupboard's a wreck."

"But could it have been anything else?" Roddy said.

"Well, it might have been another ghost," William said. "It ain't impossible, is it?"

"What? At school?" Tessa cried.

"Why not?" William said. He floated around the room and then sat on the top of the wardrobe. "I got a funny feeling somefink's happening in this whole area."

"What d'you mean?" Roddy said.

William frowned and pushed back his big cap.

"I dunno, mate. I just kept getting a feeling. Like I was *drawn* to this place, this whole area, not just the village. Know what I mean?"

"Drawn to it?" Tessa said.

"As if ... you know ... as if somefink was pulling me along with it," William said. "Course, the Ghost Hunter was on me trail, an' all. But there was somefink else as well. That I do know!"

Tessa glanced at Roddy.

"So you really think that what was going on in Mrs Justin's room could be another ghost?" Roddy said.

"Might be," William said. He floated down to a glass of water and dived into it.

"Hey," Roddy said. "I was going to drink that!"

"Just taking a little bath, mate. I ain't never 'ad a bath."

"What? Never?"

"Nar, we didn't 'ave baths at my 'ouse. We was too poor. And even poorer after me dad was took away."

William got out and shook himself.

"You're not supposed to bathe fully clothed!" Tessa said.

"Ain't you?" William said. "Well, I ain't getting undressed. No fear!"

Roddy and Tessa laughed.

"You know somefink, though," William said seriously, "I would love to meet up with another ghost, I would. I mean, me own kind. I ain't seen a ghost for years. Not since me old pal was took. Bottled. Yeah, and I don't feel easy any more neither. Not since that GIV came in that parcel. Not since Mrs Croker escaped!"

"Listen," Tessa said. "D'you think Mrs Croker and that De-Sniff are connected?"

"I don't know," Roddy said. "He could have been quite innocent."

"Yeah, but at that time of night?"

"Maybe Mrs Croker gave him some cock-and-bull story about it having to be delivered late. That sort of thing. It's possible, isn't it?"

"Yeah, mate," William said. "However it was done, it's got me rattled, I can tell you. 'Cause it means that there's somebody out there who can get at me and that is the worst thing ... the worst thing ever."

Chapter 6

Strange Things at School

When Mrs Justin entered the science lab for the last lesson of the day, she glanced cautiously round the room to see that everything was still standing. She half expected the cupboards to be wrenched from the wall and the desks to be overturned.

Wally Crabbe put up his hand.

"I've been thinking, Miss."

"Oh really, Wally?" Mrs Justin said.

"Doesn't sound like Wally," Roddy whispered to William who was snoozing in his pencil-case.

"Yeah, Miss. I been thinking about the other day," Wally Crabbe said. "I reckon this classroom's haunted!"

"That's enough of that, Wally! I don't want to

hear any more about it. I accept that there was something a bit unusual when the cupboard moved, but it really was probably a slight earth tremor. I've discussed it with Mr Witt and he agrees. So kindly be quiet, Wally," Mrs Justin said sharply.

"But it *has* to be haunted!" Wally said. "We ought to move out of here, Miss!"

"That's quite enough!" Mrs Justin snapped. Her face twitched with aggravation. Her large spectacles steamed up.

"But Miss!" Wally persisted. "I was in here early this morning."

"Oh?" Mrs Justin said with surprise. She took her specs off and wiped them vigorously on her neck scarf.

"Yeah. And while I was doing my homework..."

"You're supposed to do *that* at home!" Mrs Justin muttered.

"Yeah, but Miss," Wally continued, "while I was doing it, something sort of moved over there!" He turned in his seat and pointed at the wall where a couple of old, framed certificates dangled from their hooks.

All eyes swung towards the wall.

"What d'you mean, *moved*?" Mrs Justin said

nervously. Her neck had turned bright red and mottled like a turkey's. Then she controlled herself. "I think you're just being a little bit too over-imaginative," she added. "It's quite understandable after what occurred the other day. But now I really think we should get down to some work."

Mrs Justin looked at her lesson notes. Everyone was very quiet. You could have heard a pin drop or a mouse squeak. So when a scraping sound began, everyone noticed it at once.

Mrs Justin looked up over her huge spectacles. The children all looked up from their books. Then, as if they were many heads all on one neck, they swivelled round.

Wally Crabbe let out a gasp.

"They're doing it again, Miss!" he shrieked. His right arm was stretched out fully and the first finger of his hand pointed like a finger of doom to the framed certificates at the back of the classroom.

Roddy sat bolt upright in his chair, William came to attention in the pencil-case.

One of the framed certificates wobbled on its hook, then fell to the floor with an incredible smash!

Wally Crabbe leaped to his feet. "I'm not staying here!" he cried.

Mrs Justin swooned and clutched at her desk. "Sit down at once, Wally!" she hissed. "It ... it's just a ... a freak gust of wind. That's all!"

Wally stared at Mrs Justin for one second as if she was mad. "It ain't! It ain't! It must be a ... a ... ghost!"

"Amanda," Mrs Justin said nervously, "Would you go and fetch the caretaker, please?"

Amanda could scarcely take her eyes off the wall. They were almost popping out of her head like a couple of ping-pong balls. She hurried towards the door. Even before she got there, though, the other glass frame began to rattle and bump to and fro on its hook as if it too would soon fall to the floor.

"I ... I think I'd better go and get ... get ... somebody," Mrs Justin whispered. She stumbled to the door. As Amanda held it open, a pile of papers fell from the rear cupboard and thwacked to the ground in a cloud of dust.

Mrs Justin rushed through the door and immediately the rest of the class followed her. They went hurtling along the corridor like a pack of antelopes with a lion right behind them. Only Roddy remained in the room. And William, of course.

Roddy edged his way round the classroom.

"W–what's g–going on?" he stammered.

"Dunno, mate," William replied, "but I can't see no ghost. Course, there are other fings though, ain't there? Nasty fings."

Roddy shivered involuntarily. "What d'you mean?"

"Fings what you *don't* want to know about, Roddy."

"Tell me!" Roddy said.

"Dark fings even us ghosts steer clear of," William added.

"You mean, there are other spooky things about that we don't see or hear?"

"That's it, mate. Really 'orrible fings they can be."

"Let's get out of here," Roddy said.

"Hang about," William said. "I don't fink there's much to worry about. Let's just take a look before we scoot out like a couple of scalded cats, eh?"

Not wishing to seem a coward, Roddy tip-toed through the shards of glass and stood next to his friend.

Nervously, he reached out a shaking hand to the glass picture frame that was still on the wall.

Before he could touch it, the classroom door banged open.

"Oi, you! Pimple-brain. What d'you think you're doing?"

It was the caretaker, Mr Harding. Roddy nearly jumped out of his skin!

"Er ... we ... er, I mean, *I* was t–trying to find out what had happened. The frame was shaken off the wall," Roddy said.

Old Nosey narrowed his eyes and glowered at Roddy.

"You're one of them kids that just don't know when to clear off, ain't you?" Mr Harding said. "Just look at all this mess you are traipsing through. Do you think I ain't got nothing better to do than to keep cleaning up after you lot? Eh? Do you think I want to be at everybody's beck and call, cleaning up muck, cleaning up filth, washing, scrubbing, blistering my fingers to the bone? Eh? Do you? That teacher ought to be setting you lot an Hexample, but she don't. Do she?"

"I was just going," Roddy said. He made his way to the door.

"She's barking mad, that teacher," Mr Harding muttered. "She is. Barking!"

As William and Roddy went into the corridor, Mr Witt, the history teacher and head of lower school, saw Roddy.

"You boy!" he called in a cross voice. "Omm, hurry along!"

Mr Witt wore a smart black blazer with brass buttons and a badge on the breast pocket. His trousers were immaculately pressed and he wore heavy leather shoes. His face shone from scrubbing and he smelled of soap and aftershave. He led Roddy to the history room where the rest of the class were waiting.

"Omm. In here, boy. Just while Mr Harding clears up. Omm, Mrs Justin has just come into the staffroom feeling unwell. So I am taking over for her. We can discuss the history trip. If Wally Crabbe will stop his silly gabbling about spooks for a minute! Spooks indeed!" Mr Witt sighed and shook his head.

Roddy turned to wink at William. But, to Roddy's amazement, William was no longer there!

"William, where are you?" Roddy whispered.

"What's the matter, boy?" Mr Witt snapped. "Go and sit down!"

Mr Witt shut the door and started telling the class about the coming trip to Chillwood Castle.

"Omm, right," he called to everybody.

A sudden terror crossed Roddy's mind that William could have been dragged into some sort of weird ghostly underworld.

Mr Witt's voice rang out, "Roddy Oliver. Are you listening?"

"Er ... yes, sir," Roddy said.

Mr Witt's whopping great bushy eyebrows waggled up and down as he spoke enthusiastically. His damp, soft hands waved in the air as if they were made of putty.

"Omm, as you know, Chillwood Castle is on our doorstep, so to speak. It is a place of great local historic interest and especially relevant to our current topic – the Civil War!"

I can't just sit here! Roddy thought to himself. *I've got to go and find William. I've got to!*

He put up his hand.

"May I go to the toilet, sir?"

Mr Witt sighed in exasperation.

"Omm, if you *really* must," he said. He looked at his watch. "The sixth form are due in here in a minute. So we shall be moving back to the science room. Meet us there, please, Roddy.

"Right, sir."

The next minute Roddy was running back to the place where he'd last seen his ghostly friend.

Chapter 7

Fire Alarm

"William!" Roddy called as loudly as he dared. He knew he couldn't be long out of the classroom otherwise Mr Witt would send somebody after him.

"William! Where are you?"

When he got no answer, Roddy hurried along the silent corridor. There was a cloakroom on his left. On his right, more classrooms. Ahead of him were a pair of brown swing doors which led to the main entrance foyer. Footsteps were approaching from the other side of them. Roddy slipped into the cloakroom, behind a partition wall, waiting to see who it was. The footsteps got closer and closer and then went past him. Roddy peeked out. It wasn't a teacher, or the headmaster, as he'd half-expected. It was a fireman, carrying a fire-extinguisher.

Must be checking them all, Roddy thought.

He relaxed.

He was about to step out into the open but instead threw himself against the darkened wall as if he'd come face to face with a snake.

The fireman! He was *sniffing* as only one person in the world could!

It was De-Sniff, the parcel deliverer. He shuffled along the corridor in his battered old boots. His trousers with their frayed turn-ups scudded the floor. At every classroom he stopped and secretively peered in. Roddy crouched behind a huddle of coats and wondered what on earth he was up to.

He waited for De-Sniff to move away round the corner, then he ran to Tessa's classroom, knocked on the door and went in. Everybody looked up as he did so.

"Yes, Roddy?" Mr Birch said. "What can I do for you?"

"Er..." Roddy said. "Tessa's wanted on the phone, sir."

"The phone?" Mr Birch said. "Oh. Right. Tessa?"

"What's all this about?" she snapped, as soon as they got outside.

"William's missing!" Roddy said urgently. "And that De-Sniff bloke's in school. He's got a fireman's uniform on."

"Fireman?" Tessa cried.

"He scares me," Roddy said.

"You don't think he's come here after William with some more GIV, do you?"

"I don't know!" Roddy said. "It's a coincidence though, isn't it?

"Yeah," Tessa said. "What shall we do?"

"I'll go and look for William," Roddy said. "You go and keep an eye on De-Sniff."

Roddy ran to the library. He thought William might have gone there. It was the only place he could think of. But it was locked and silent. Roddy pressed his nose to the glass. At the far end, he could see a computer screen still lit up. Somebody was in there, but he couldn't see properly.

Roddy knocked on the glass.

To his amazement, William popped up, floating in the air above the computer.

Roddy gestured to him furiously. William floated

towards him. He slipped straight through the glass door and stood grinning at his friend.

"I just got fed up, mate. Don't get narked with me. I don't know what's goin' on in half of them lessons. So I thought I'd come up here and have a go on the tappers."

"You should have told me!" Roddy shouted crossly. "I thought you'd been kidnapped or something!"

"Sorry, mate. Since you showed me them games at your 'ouse, I've been wanting to have another go at 'em."

"I even got Tessa out of her classroom!" Roddy yelled. "That De-Sniff bloke is here."

"What? In school?"

"Yeah. Dressed up like a fireman."

William's eyebrows twitched off his face. His eyeballs popped out of his head. "Where is 'e now?"

"I don't know," Roddy said. "He was looking in all the classrooms. We've got to find out what he's up to!"

They soon found De-Sniff. But there was no sign of Tessa.

Roddy and William watched the grubby man

carefully. He was now outside the science lab, where Mr Witt had taken Roddy's class.

"He's smiling to himself!" Roddy whispered.

De-Sniff knocked on the classroom door and went in. Roddy and William got close enough to peer into the room.

"Omm, yes? Can I help you?" Mr Witt was saying.

"Sniff – sniff. I'm just testing!" De-Sniff said.

"Testing?" Mr Witt began to look cross. "You can't..."

But De-Sniff took no notice. Without speaking, he stood in the front of the class and began to undo the knob on the top of his fire-extinguisher.

"You simply can't just barge in here and start testing...!" Mr Witt said. He threw his hands up in dismay. De-Sniff took no notice. His fingers were moving quickly on the black knob of the extinguisher and his eyes were searching the children's faces before him. Suddenly, a terrific spurt of spray gushed out of the fire-extinguisher and De-Sniff pointed the nozzle at the children. It showered all over the room and all over them.

"Stop it!" Mr Witt belowed. "Stop it at once!"

But De-Sniff turned round and as he did so the

white foam shot out all over Mr Witt, nearly knocking him over. Mr Witt's hands went up to his face. He gasped in astonishment. De-Sniff pretended he couldn't switch the extinguisher off. The children were shrieking and screaming – some with laughter. A few had already begun to flick foam at each other. De-Sniff just kept turning round and round spraying everywhere in the room. Roddy stayed just long enough to see Mr Witt covered from head to foot in white foam, like the abominable snowman.

"Let's get out of here," he said. "Unless I'm mistaken, that isn't real foam. It's Ghost Immobilizing Vapour disguised as foam. He must know it's my class and he's hoping you're there with me! He's trying to get you!"

"Where's Tessa?" William, said.

"I don't know," Roddy replied, "but one thing I do know. We've got to get you out of here, fast!"

Tessa was outside. She hadn't found De-Sniff. But as she crept round a corner of the building, she spotted an old white van. On the side of it, somebody had painted: *Fire Service*.

Tessa looked carefully about her. There was

nobody around. Nobody in the playground, nobody near the van. She went closer and peered inside the cab. There was nobody sitting in it. She went round the back of it. One of its doors was open. Tessa couldn't resist peeping in. It had some strange-looking jars and other equipment in there and right inside, a large box. Tessa glanced over her shoulder, scanning the playground once more. Then she stepped up into the back of the van and pulled the door half closed behind her. She made her way deep into the van and opened the box. Inside it was a spray gun and on it the letters: GIV.

Tessa was just closing the lid when her heart gave a lurch. Outside, there were hurrying footsteps and loud sniffing. She tried to scramble to the door to get out. But even as she did so, De-Sniff scurried into view. She ducked down. The back doors of the van were hurriedly slammed shut. De-Sniff climbed into the driver's seat, started the engine and drove the van like a maniac all over the grass towards the school's exit. As he did so, he knocked over and squashed Old Nosey's Keep Off The Grass sign. Then, to Tessa's horror, he drove the van out of the school gates and roared down the road. Through the rear window, she briefly caught sight of Mr Witt as he rushed out into the playground, waving his arms furiously. He was covered from head to foot in white foam. He was also very, very angry.

Tessa crouched down. Her mind was racing. *He'll go to the village shop. Then I'll jump out*, she thought. But De-Sniff drove straight past the shop and Tessa realized they were heading down a very dark and dingy little lane, amongst weird, spindly trees.

The van bounced around as it hit potholes and swayed from side to side. But eventually it stopped. De-Sniff's door banged shut. Tessa grabbed a spanner that was lying in the back of the van. She intended to defend herself. She pulled an old rug across her, hoping it would cover her. She reckoned if she could leap up and surprise him, she might get a chance to run away before he knew what had happened. And if she didn't, if he tried to harm her, she'd fight! Her heart was knocking against her ribs. Her breath was tight in her throat.

She listened tensely.

Footsteps! She heard them. Shuffle, shuffle. She heard him sniff loudly and spit. She heard him drum his fingers on the metal of the van as if he was thinking. She gripped the spanner very tight, so tight her hands began to sweat. Then she heard the footsteps again. She was coiled up like a spring, ready to explode as soon as he came near her.

But De-Sniff didn't come. She heard him trudging away from the van, whistling to himself. Whistling an idiotic tune. A repetitive tune. Tessa waited. Then she threw aside the rug. The knuckles on her hands were white and she was wet through with sweat. At last she stood up. Cautiously she unfastened the back door and got out. Just ahead of her, she could see an old, filthy caravan. She crept down the side of the van, noticing a grubby mobile telephone on the driver's seat.

Very softly, *so* softly, she opened the door of the van and picked the phone up. She hugged it to her chest like a life-line. Then she tip-toed across open ground towards the safety of the wood. She leant against a tree and tapped out a number. The telephone began to ring.

"Hello?"

It was Roddy's voice.

"Roddy! Listen, it's me."

"Tessa? Where are you?" he cried.

"I got in De-Sniff's van. Accidentally. I'm at a place where he's got a caravan..."

Suddenly a hand clapped across Tessa's mouth. It was a grimy, slimy hand. Her arm was bent up her back. The telephone went dead.

"Got you!" De-Sniff gloated. "Got you, you stinking little snooper! Got you, good and proper!"

Chapter 8

Trapped!

De-Sniff hurled Tessa into the inner cave of Mrs Croker's hide-out.

She stayed huddled on the floor as the tall figure in the long cape turned and glowered at her. Mrs Croker's nose quivered like the proboscis of an ant-eater.

"I caught her snoopin', guv, I did. Out there. I brought her in here to you straight away, boss." He looked at Mrs Croker hoping for praise. He was sweating with the effort of shoving Tessa and big damp rings spread under his armpits.

"How did you get here?" The Ghost Hunter hissed. Her eyes blazed like two gun barrels.

"In the van, boss," De-Sniff said. "I saw her creep out. She must have got in when I was at that school."

"Tie her up!" Mrs Croker snapped. "She'll come in useful as bait. The sort of bait you put on a hook when you want to catch a big fish. And who will come to take the bait. Eh?"

De-Sniff grinned.

"Right, boss," he said. He grabbed Tessa roughly by the arms and soon had her trussed up like a Christmas turkey.

"You won't get away with it!" Tessa yelled at her. "The police will come!"

"The police!" Mrs Croker sneered. "Gag the sickly, whingeing little brat."

De-Sniff pulled a filthy cotton handkerchief out of his pocket. It was covered in old bogeys and oil. He tied it round Tessa's mouth.

"That'll shut your cake hole," De-Sniff sniggered. "Right little trombone, ain't you? Always blasting off, ain't you? Got more to say than you got to eat, ain't you?"

Tessa stared at him and struggled. But he only laughed at her.

"You won't get out of them ropes, Miss. I done 'em good and tight."

"Did anyone follow you, Sniff?" Mrs Croker whispered.

"No, boss."

"Does anyone know she's here?"

"No boss. She was trying to talk to somebody on that old phone, but she didn't because I got me hand over her gob first. Just like that, boss!"

Mrs Croker looked at De-Sniff and sneered.

"Right," she said. "Unload the van. And look sharp about it! We haven't got all week. We've got work to do!"

"We need to go and get some more of that chemical you need for the GIV, boss. Sometime."

Mrs Croker looked up and nodded.

"A bit later then," she said. "I'm working on this Ghost Detecting Compass. It worked perfectly to get me here. Perfectly! But it needs some refinements. Another of my wonderful inventions, De-Sniff!"

"Oh yes, boss," De-Sniff said. "It's brilliant. You come up with some weird and incredible things, you do."

De-Sniff went out of the cavern, leaving Tessa in a corner on a mouldy, smelly and moth-eaten quilt. Mrs Croker went on working at her work bench. It was cold down there and Tessa was terrified that Roddy and William would never, ever find her.

* * *

Roddy was pacing all round his bedroom.

"She's captured, William, that's what!"

"Tell us then, mate. What did she say?"

"That she had got into De–Sniff's van at school, he had driven off with her in the back and she was at a caravan somewhere. And then the phone went dead!" He looked at William. "I'm scared."

"Yeah. I know what you mean," William murmured. "She's with De–Sniff, so that means she's probably with the Ghost 'Unter an' all, don't it?" William was shaking with fear.

"We've got to find her!" Roddy shouted. "We've just got to!"

He stopped pacing. He snapped his fingers.

"There's a caravan site not far away! It's called Happy Days Caravan Park. Maybe she's there. It's the only place round here where there are caravans." He turned to William. "Come on, let's go and take a look."

"Not me," William said nervously. "Not me, mate, please..."

"What d'you mean, not you?"

"I just don't want to go. It's too dangerous."

"Huh!" Roddy snapped angrily. "You don't mean to tell me you're going to just sit here!"

"You go, mate. 'Ere, take a brush. But make sure you put it in your bag if you see Croker."

Roddy snatched the brush from William's hand. He glared at the shoe–shine boy.

"She's in trouble, William! She needs us!"

"I know that. An' I wouldn't hesitate. Not normally. But the Ghost 'Unter, Roddy."

"Get lost," Roddy said. He thought himself upwards and flew straight through the bedroom wall and over Little Henlock as fast as he could go.

He reached a field which was covered with caravans. There were small roads in between them. Many had cars or vans parked next to them. Roddy landed and put the brush away in his shoulder bag.

As he walked along the narrow tarmac road, he looked to see if he could spot the white van. He walked right round the whole site, but he couldn't see it. Then he saw a man cleaning his motorbike. He went over to him.

"Excuse me," he said. "I'm looking for my sister. She's got red hair."

The man shook his head.

"She came here in a white van."

"Sorry. I haven't seen any girls today. There's not been many folk about."

Roddy went farther on down the site. He was jittery and angry with William and he didn't know what to do next.

Suddenly somebody tapped his shoulder. Roddy spun round and saw William grinning sat him.

"Sorry, mate," he said. "I wasn't finkin' properly. I was only finkin' of meself. Any luck?"

"No," Roddy said. "But she did say a caravan and this is the only caravan park in the whole area."

"No, it ain't," William said. "I just seen an old caravan – blimey, it were an' old crate an' all. Back there."

"Where?" Roddy yelled.

"Just over that hill. I flew over it. It's in a kind of wooded place. But I don't fink it'll be the one, Roddy. It was fallin' to bits!"

"Never mind," Roddy snapped. "Show me. Show me now!"

As Roddy grabbed the brush, William zoomed into the air and flew ahead. They soon reached the hidden caravan. There was no sign of De–Sniff's van.

They circled the whole place.

"What d'you fink?" William said nervously.

"There's nobody there," Roddy said. "But let's take a closer look."

"Nah," William said. "It ain't worth it, mate. Look, it's deserted!"

Roddy ignored William, though, and flew down to the ground. He went right up to the caravan and looked inside.

"Somebody lives here, anyway," he said.

They turned and searched around.

"Look," Roddy said. "Tyre tracks. And they're new ones."

"I don't like it, Roddy," William said. "I got a bad feeling about it. She ain't here. Is she?"

"Come over here," Roddy shouted. He pointed to the ground. "What's that?"

William looked closely. They were at the top of the steps leading down to Mrs Croker's hide-out.

"What?" William said.

Roddy bent down and picked up a hair band.

"It's Tessa's," he whispered.

Roddy stuffed his shoe-brush back into his bag and went slowly down the steps. William followed. Roddy opened the door to the underground hide-out.

"We've got to take a look!" he hissed when William shook his head.

Roddy stepped into the dark, damp place and

William followed. They moved slowly, carefully through the dank, rotting cavern. Water dripped about them. Crawly things moved away from their footsteps. Eventually they reached another door.

"Don't go in there," William whispered. "It's probably a trap!"

Roddy gave the door a gentle push, ready to spring back and run for it if anything happened. The door opened quietly. He pushed it further until he could poke his head round it. As he did so, he gasped and rushed forwards.

"Tess!" he cried.

"Oh, thank goodness you came!" she yelled. "Thank goodness!"

Roddy quickly untied her.

"Mrs Croker and De-Sniff done this?" William said.

"Yeah," Tessa said. She got stiffly to her feet and held on to Roddy. "Ouch. I'm numb. But, we've got to get out of here! They've only just nipped out! They'll be back. Soon!"

"Are you sure you're OK?" Roddy said.

"Just about." She tried to walk but her legs were so stiff she had to hold on to Roddy for a few moments.

William was gliding towards another door.

"Come on," Roddy called him. "Let's get out of here!"

But William said, "There's somefink 'ere, Roddy. Somefink I got to see!"

"They've been going in and out of there," Tessa said.

Something seemed to be drawing William to the room. Drawing him forward. Leading him.

"Let's just take a peep, then," Roddy said. "There might be something we ought to know about."

They followed William to the doorway and stared, open mouthed.

"Oh, no!" William hissed. "Will you take a look at that?"

A huge array of bottles, row upon row, stood against the far wall. And in each bottle moved a shrunken ghost. Some of the ghosts clawed at the jars to be let out. Others sat on their haunches with their heads in their hands.

"It's terrible!" Tessa cried.

Tears streamed down William's face as he looked at the poor trapped ghosts.

"Is there anything we can do?" Roddy said.

As he moved forwards, Tessa froze.

"There's somebody coming!" she snapped. "Listen!"

The main door creaked and banged shut. Footsteps, rapid footsteps sounded, striding down through the main cavern towards them.

"He's *here*! I can smell the beastly creature! He's here, De-Sniff! We've got him!" shrieked the Ghost Hunter.

"Quick, William!" Roddy shouted. "Give Tessa a brush!"

William grabbed at a brush, but in his haste, it slipped from his hand and slid under a cupboard. Roddy dived on to the floor to get it.

At the same instant, the door to the inner cave burst open and Mrs Croker stood there, glowering triumphantly.

"Oh, yes!" she screamed. "Now I've got you!"

Chapter 9

The Solstice

The Ghost Hunter's nose trembled violently in anticipation of bottling William. She had been after him for so long. So long! And now, here he was, fallen straight into her hands.

"The Ghost Immobilizing Vapour!" she snapped at De-Sniff. "Give it to me!"

De-Sniff turned pale.

"B-but I-I ain't got it, boss. I left it in the van, I did. I-I didn't think we'd be needing it – not here, I didn't!"

Mrs Croker swung round on him. Her eyes blazed at him.

"You blithering dolt!" she snarled and threw out her huge cape, making herself seem like a great dark bird of prey.

Roddy's fingers closed on the brush under the cupboard. He jumped to his feet.

William came to his senses. He grabbed Tessa by the hand and yanked her forwards.

"Come on!" he yelled. "Come on!"

Mrs Croker lashed out at De-Sniff and sent him sprawling across the floor of the cave. Then she lunged at the children with all her force. But William, Tessa and Roddy, running towards her, passed straight through and vanished into thin air.

"I've lost him! Again! I've lost him!" Mrs Croker wailed. "You blockhead. You dimwit! You numbskull!"

De-Sniff cowered in a corner.

"I didn't think, boss," he whined. "I didn't think he'd be here, did I?"

"You *should* have thought, you snivelling, useless termite!"

"Well, it wasn't my fault," De-Sniff muttered. "How am I supposed to know?"

"Shut up!" Mrs Croker scowled. She shook with anger and disappointment. Then her gaze fell on the array of ghosts she'd already got in bottles.

"Come on, De-Sniff, you article. Get up! We've

got work to do now. Very, very urgent work! We've got to pack up. Everything! Again!"

"Everything, boss?" De-Sniff said wearily.

"Yes! Everything!" Mrs Croker snarled. "And it's all your fault!"

"That was too close," Roddy said.

"Yeah," William murmured. "I ... I thought she'd got me!"

"We ought to ring the police," Tessa said.

"They'd never believe us," Roddy said.

"And what'd happen to all those ghosts what she's got fastened up in them 'orrible bottles? Eh? If the police came they might smash them or chuck them away."

"Or put them in a museum," Roddy said. "More likely. And then they'd never get free."

"That Mrs Croker," William said. "She's off her blinkin' 'ead."

"She's raving," Tessa said. "When I was tied up, she kept going on to that De-Sniff about the evening of the solstice or something ... saying she absolutely knew it was the TIME and that she'd been drawn to the area by using some sort of Ghost Detecting Compass which she'd invented!"

"*Ghost Detecting Compass?*" William said. "Never heard of it."

"And what's a solstice?" Roddy added.

"I don't know," Tessa said. "Let's ask Mum. She might know, especially if it's something to do with weird goings-on."

"Mum," Tessa said. "What's a solstice?"

Mr Oliver, who happened to be passing, carrying a plank of wood, called over his shoulder, "A solstice is like a poultice, only hotter!"

"Very funny, Dad," Roddy said.

"A solstice?" Mrs Oliver cried, turning towards them from her computer. "You must be psychic, dear. I was just writing something about that for my article!"

"Oh?" Tessa said.

"A solstice," Mrs Oliver went on, "is the time when the sun reaches its highest point – its zenith. It only happens twice a year and in olden times it used to be the time of great mystery and rituals – you know, like Stonehenge and all that."

"So, it's important?" Roddy said.

"Oh yes, it is. To some people it's very important."

"Well, when is it?" Tessa said.

"June the twenty-first," Mrs Oliver said.

"That's the day after tomorrow!" Roddy gasped.

"Yes," Mrs Oliver replied. "But don't get too excited. It won't affect us. At least, not much."

"Oh, no?" Roddy muttered.

As they went back up to his room, Tessa said, "I think we need to go back to the hide-out on the twenty-first."

"You *must* be joking!" William cried.

"We've got to see what she's up to," Tessa said. "It's the only way we'll ever get a chance of beating her and saving those poor, wretched bottled ghosts! It was awful to see them. And we need to know just why the evening of the solstice is so important to her!"

"She's right," Roddy said. "But the only thing is it's the Chillwood Castle trip the day after tomorrow. There's no way I'll get out of that!"

"And I'm supposed to be revising all day," Tessa added. "I've got exams coming up and I've got a study day."

"It'll just have to wait until we get back from Chillwood. And then we'll have to try and go in the evening and have a snoop. That's all we can do!"

"In the meantime," Tessa said, "we've all got to be on our guard and watch out for De-Sniff and Mrs Croker!"

Chapter 10

Skull in Room D

By lunchtime the next day, the only stranger Roddy and William had encountered in the school was the new nit nurse.

As Roddy strolled along the corridor to the dining hall, he passed his formroom. Sitting at her desk with her head in her hands was Mrs Justin. Roddy poked his head round the door. Mrs Justin looked up quickly.

"Are you OK, Mrs Justin?" Roddy asked.

Mrs Justin sighed. "More or less," she said.

"There've been some weird goings on, haven't there, Miss?"

"Yes, Roddy. Most weird!"

"Well, don't worry, Miss," Roddy said. "See you later."

"I don't think I'm taking your class today," Mrs Justin said.

"Mr Witt said you were taking us for drama, because Mrs Flight is away."

"Oh, am I?" Mrs Justin said. "Standing in for Mrs Flight, you say? Oh yes, I remember. After lunch, isn't it?"

"No, *last* lesson this afternoon, Mrs Justin," Roddy said.

"Oh yes, thank you, Roddy!"

"Blimey," William said as they carried on down the corridor, "she's going off 'er trolley, ain't she?"

"She's under strain," Roddy said. "There couldn't really be something *horrible* working in there, could there?"

"Well, I ain't seen anyfink," William said. "But I'll keep the old peepers open."

The boys started to relax once they reached the last lesson of the day.

"It's going dark quick tonight, ain't it?" William said.

"Yeah," Roddy said. He glanced out of the window at the dark swirling clouds. "It's brewing up for a storm."

The lights were on in room D and the curtains were drawn. It made the drama room seem very snug – just right to do acting in. There was a small raised area at one end, which was curtained off at the moment. The class was to do its drama in the main part of the room.

"Let's ... er ... let's start with ... an improvisation," Mrs Justin said, as if fumbling for ideas. She paused for a moment, as if waiting for inspiration. "Yes, imagine you've each been given an ice-cream and it's very hot – the sun that is, not the ice-cream – and you have to eat it very fast."

Roddy had just started licking at his imaginary ice-cream, when the lights started flickering.

"What's that?" Wally Crabbe said.

"It's just the power lines," Mrs Justin said quickly. "The wind's getting up outside."

It was true. A howling wind was pounding at the windows.

"Carry on," Mrs Justin said, raising her voice.

The children continued trying to eat imaginary ice-creams.

Suddenly, a tremendous clap of thunder boomed overhead.

"I don't like thunder, Miss!" one of the children cried, nervously.

Mrs Justin looked worried. She lifted a curtain at one of the windows. The sky flashed with lightning. Mrs Justin turned back to the children.

"I know it's exciting," she said hesitantly, "but we really must carry on with our lesson."

"Miss..." Wally Crabbe put his hand halfway up. His face looked puzzled, then plain scared. He pointed at the stage area.

Something had appeared between the curtains of the small stage. The whole class turned towards it.

A human skull with a pair of crimson eyes burning in its bony sockets stared across the room. The class hushed instantly.

Then the skull whispered, "Mrs Jus – tin. Mrs Jus – tin!"

The lights flickered frantically and went off.

Some of the children screamed. Others huddled together in panic. A second later, the lights came on again. The skull had gone. Mrs Justin stood rooted to the spot. Then she slowly crumpled to the floor.

Roddy jumped towards the curtains and tore them open. Wally Crabbe and others ran to the door and bolted. Roddy looked behind the curtains at the stage.

He stared up at the ceiling. There was nothing, absolutely nothing there.

"Fetch Mr Witt," Amanda Bates yelled to one of her terrified pals as she leaned over Mrs Justin.

Mr Witt and Amanda brought Mrs Justin round and then led her away to the staffroom. The other children were told to go to Mr Witt's room. But Roddy waited behind.

"'Ere, mate," William said. "Come and have a gander at this, will you?" Roddy stared at the area of the floor William was pointing at. He bent down and examined it.

"It's mud, isn't it?"

"Look a bit closer," William said.

Roddy got right down on his hands and knees.

"Pooh, it stinks."

"Yeah. What of?" William said.

"Polish?" Roddy said.

"That's it, mate. Now look a bit closer. What else can you see?"

Roddy searched the floor intently.

"There's a sort of mark in it, isn't there?'

"Yeah, an' guess what."

"What?"

"That mark is part of a shoe-print."

"So you think...?"

William went to the back of the stage area. "Just come over 'ere!" he called. He pointed to a series of lines which formed a rectangle in the floor.

"A trap door!" Roddy gasped.

"Take a brush," William said, "and let's have a look."

Roddy and William passed straight through the trapdoor, down some steps. They found themselves in an underground storeroom.

William led Roddy along a passageway until they came to another set of steps. "Up there," he said.

They floated up the steps. At the top of them was a door set in a wall.

"Where are we?" Roddy said.

"Don't you know, mate?" William said.

"No," Roddy said. "Where?"

William floated slowly through the door. Roddy followed, wondering where on earth his ghostly friend was leading him. As they emerged on the other side, Roddy understood.

They were in the caretaker's room.

"You think Old Nosey had something to do with the skull?" Roddy gasped.

William tapped the side of his nose. It bounced about and twitched like a fish's tail.

The room was deserted. The caretaker's newspaper was neatly folded on the table. The broom stood against a door.

"It could be coincidence," Roddy said. "Old Nosey is always about the school, you know. He's bound to have cleaned the floor in the drama room."

"Yeah?" William said. "Well, let's have a peek."

"OK," Roddy said.

As they started searching the room, Roddy heard footsteps coming down the corridor. He told William and they both shrank to the size of peas.

It was Old Nosey. He came into the room, plonked himself down on his chair and grabbed the newspaper.

"Wonder how long he's going to stick around for?" Roddy said.

"Sh," William said. "Someone else is coming."

Wally Crabbe burst in.

"Uncle Jake!" he gasped.

Old Nosey put down his newspaper.

"What's the matter, Wally? You look like you've seen a ghost."

"D–don't talk to me about ghosts, Uncle Jake," Wally stammered. "They're scaring me daft."

"What ghosts are you on about?" Old Nosey asked.

"The ones in the science lab and room D," Wally shrieked. "There was a skull with glowing red eyes!"

The caretaker started to laugh.

Wally looked hurt.

"It's not funny, Uncle Jake!"

"I think you'll see the funny side," Old Nosey said, "when I've told you the whole story!"

"What d'you mean?"

"There are no *ghosts*, Wally! Just me, your old Uncle!"

"You!" cried Wally. "You, Uncle Jake?"

"Yes, just me playing a few tricks on our friend Mrs Justin."

"She's not *my* friend," Wally growled. "She picks on me all the time."

"Exactly," Old Nosey said. "She's no friend of mine, either. But maybe if she thinks this school's spooked, she'll be looking for a new job, like. Eh?"

Old Nosey put a finger to the side of his overgrown nose and smirked.

"Oh, I get it," Walley said, grinning now. "Nice one, Uncle Jake!"

"Come on, Wally," Old Nosey said. "Let's get you a bar of chocolate from the machine. To get over your fright, eh?"

"Yeah! Thanks!" Wally said. He and the caretaker left the room, just as William popped out through the keyhole of a locked cupboard. He was grinning all over his cheeky face.

"What?" Roddy said.

"The skull's in there, all right," William said. "And somefink else. Somefink what is very convincing!"

"It's there?" Roddy shrieked. "So we've got *proof* Old Nosey is up to tricks!"

"Not 'alf," William said. "I fink it'd be a good idea if you go and fetch Mr Witt down 'ere."

"Now?" Roddy said.

"As quick as you can," William said.

"What else is there to see, besides the skull?" Roddy said.

"I'll show you everyfink when you've got Mr Witt!" William said. "But 'urry up, in case Old Nosey comes back. We don't want 'im destroying the evidence or nuffink, do we?"

Roddy gave William the shoe-brush and became visible again.

"I just hope Mr Witt will come," Roddy said.

He snatched open the door of the caretaker's room and walked straight into Old Nosey.

Chapter 11

In the Caretaker's Room

The bell rang loud and long for the end of school. Tessa came out of her classroom and made her way through the throng of children towards the cloakroom. As she put on her coat, she listened to her friend, Catherine.

"Yes," Catherine said. "I'm going to a gig tomorrow. It's Blue Heaven and I'm..."

Catherine turned round. A puzzled expression passed over her face.

"Tessa?" she said. "Tessa? Well, really! She didn't even wait!"

Tessa was in fact still standing next to her. But invisibly. William had just pushed a brush into her hand.

"What's the matter, William?" Tessa cried.

"Go and get Mr Witt!" William said. "Bring him to Old Nosey's room! He's got Roddy there ... and there's something else he's got to see before it's too late!"

He took the brush back from Tessa and flew off. Immediately she became visible.

Catherine, who had just made her way to the exit, caught sight of her.

"Tessa? Where were you?"

"Oh ... er ... I ... was just here!" she said. "Just hanging about. Er, see you tomorrow."

Tessa barged past her friend and ran to find Mr Witt. He was sitting in the staffroom, about to have a cup of tea.

"You've got to come, sir!" Tessa said. "It's urgent!"

Mr Witt said, "Omm," but Tessa kept pestering him.

"Sir ... *please*!" she said.

Mr Witt put his cup and saucer down. He muttered under his breath, but soon found himself hurrying after Tessa.

"Now you tell me, you little creep, what was you doing in my room? Eh?"

Old Nosey had Roddy by the ear and was almost lifting him off the floor by it. He pushed his own face with its big boily nose right up to Roddy's.

"Ouch!" Roddy cried. "Let go!"

But Old Nosey didn't let go.

"I've a good mind to swing you round by this ear and use you to dust the cobwebs off of them walls. D'you hear me, Oliver? I've just about had enough of you and all the litter you drop and all the cheek you give me! You ain't got any respect for your elders and betters, have you, you little bag of flea pellets! You're like a lot of hig-nor-amous boys I've got to know over the years, Oliver. And I hate 'em! Boys like you, Oliver, ought to be taken out to sea in a big ship and dumped in Davy Jones's Locker. Dumped in and locked up until you was old enough to show a bit of respect!"

"Let's go!" Roddy said. "My ear's coming off. Ouch!"

As he shouted, William came back into the room. Suddenly the broom lifted itself up from a corner of the room and whacked against the cupboard. Mr Harding turned, sharply. He let go of Roddy's ear.

"What ... what was that?" he said nervously.

The door to Mr Harding's room burst open at

that moment and standing there were Mr Witt and Tessa.

Mr Witt looked at the caretaker. Then at Roddy who was rubbing his ear. Then at Tessa.

"Omm, what's all this about?" he said.

"Sir." Roddy shouted. "Tell Mr Harding to open his cupboard!"

"What?" Mr Witt said. "What is going on?"

"This 'oly little 'orror has been in my room. He's bin searching through my things, that's what!" Old Nosey growled.

"Tell him to open the cupboard, sir!" Roddy pleaded. "The skull ... the skull. It's in there!"

"What are you talking about?" Mr Witt asked, confused.

"He's been in my cupboard, that's proof!" Old Nosey insisted.

"Wait a minute, Mr Harding. Now listen to me. Have you been snooping around in Mr Harding's room? Yes or no?"

"Well, yes sir, but..."

"Never mind *but*..." Mr Witt said. "This is a serious matter, boy!"

"But, sir!" Tessa said. "The skull!"

"Be quiet, Tessa," Mr Witt cut across. "I've just

about had enough about ghosts and skulls and all that nonsense!"

"Oh no!" William muttered. " 'E ain't gonna listen, is 'e? Right then. I'll just have to bloomin' well show 'im, won't I?"

William flew towards Old Nosey's cupboard and went into it through the keyhole. Once inside, he began to kick at the door with all his might.

"What the dickens is that?" said Mr Witt.

Suddenly the door burst open and on to the floor rolled – the skull. It landed on its back with its two red eyes staring up at Mr Witt.

Mr Witt gasped. "Omm, what on earth is this?" He turned to Mr Harding.

"I – I don't know nothing about it!" Old Nosey said. "These kids must have put it there!"

"We did not!" Tessa shouted hotly. "You put it there yourself!"

"And you scared Mrs Justin with it!" Roddy added. "You've really got it in for her!"

Before Old Nosey could say another word, William went back into the cupboard, right to the back of it and called to Roddy.

"Look, sir," Roddy shouted. "There's a lever here which pulls a string! It must make those glass frames move in the science room! And there's a hole in the back here where he could push and shake that cupboard in the classroom as well."

"What are you saying, Roddy?" Mr Witt said.

"That Mr Harding has been trying to scare the wits out of Mrs Justin so he could get rid of her. He hates clearing up her messy room all the time. And the way she goes on at his nephew. Look, this is how he jiggled the certificate frames and moved our cupboard."

Mr Witt glared angrily at the caretaker. Old Nosey knew he was trapped.

"It was only a *bit of fun*," he said in a weaselly voice. "I didn't think she'd take it serious, like. You know me, a bit of a jokester, I am."

"I see," Mr Witt said. "Right. Tessa and Roddy, you can go now. I'll deal with this matter. Off you go!"

As soon as they were outside, William said, "Here, catch hold of a brush. We ain't gonna stay out here just when old Bumper Conk gets his comeuppance, are we?"

Invisibly the three of them passed back through the closed door of Old Nosey's room.

"So you see, Mr Witt, it weren't at all like them

blessed kids would have you believe – little liars they are. Honest. They are, really, sir. They'm always givin' me trouble, 'specially that Roddy Oliver boy. He's a right nuisance he is, Mr Witt."

"Oh?"

"I mean, I am really sorry if I done anything to upset Mrs Justin, I didn't mean to, not nohow. But them kids, they are the limit. And to be quite honest and candid with you, sir, I have been thinking of leaving this job. After all the time I put in an' all. They drop litter, give me lip and all sorts they do. It's really difficult to put up with it all sometimes. And you seen for yourself how they came in my very own room. Snooping around. No, sir, I just can't put up with it much longer."

"Omm now, Mr Harding, I'm sure things aren't so bad," Mr Witt said. "Come along, now. We don't want to lose you. Surely it's all a bit of a mistake, shall we say? An error of judgement?"

"Oh ... oh yes, it was, sir, and you can take it from me. It won't never happen again. But them kids. It was mostly them to blame. In the end."

"Mmm. Right. I see your point, Mr Harding. And I will have a word. Yes."

"Thank you very much, Mr Witt. I do appreciate your concern. I do indeed. Really I do."

"Yuk!" Tessa growled. "Let's get out before I throw up!"

"Blimey," William shouted. "It's enough to make you cringe, ain't it?"

"Cringe?" Roddy said. "If I hear much more, I'll break down and weep for Old Nosey. He's had such a hard time, hasn't he?"

Chapter 12

Chillwood Castle

When Roddy came down to breakfast, William was shrunk to the size of a teaspoon and was sitting on the rim of the milk-jug.

"Do you mind!" Roddy said. "Your boots are dangling over the milk!"

Mrs Oliver turned from the sink and stared at Roddy.

"What are you talking about?" she said.

"Oh ... er ... it's a poem, Mum," Roddy said. He'd forgotten she was in the kitchen. Of course, she couldn't see William at all.

"A poem?" Mrs Oliver said.

"Er, yeah," Roddy said. "Er ... your boots are dangling over the milk and cows are dangling over the moon, er ... soon you'll be sweeping up with a silver broom."

Roddy's mother shook her head.

"Hoping to be Poet Laureate, are you?" She went into the hall to call Mr Oliver who was still in bed.

"Sorry, mate," William said. "I keep forgetting, see, that you lot have to eat. I mean, I hope you don't fink I ain't got no manners."

"Mmm," Roddy said, lifting up the jug. "Would you mind moving?" He poured milk over his breakfast.

Tessa came in.

"Oh, Roddy, you're *so gross*!" she said, seeing Roddy's mouth crammed full of cereal.

"I..." Roddy began.

"Stop! Don't speak! You're spluttering bits all over the table!" She looked round the room. "Where's William?"

Roddy pointed to a cornflake bobbing up and down on the tablecloth. Then he swallowed the mouthful of food he'd been chewing.

"He's in shrink mode," Roddy said.

"Who's taking you to Chillwood today?" Tessa asked.

"Omm, Mr Witt. Omm, omm, of course." Roddy laughed.

Tessa flicked back her long, red hair. Then she

whispered, "Well, just be careful! De-Sniff might be following us around."

The cornflake stopped bobbing up and down on the table cloth. William grew back to his full size.

"He won't know anyfink about the trip to Chillwood Castle though, will he?" he said.

"You never know," Roddy whispered. He turned to Tessa. "We'll be careful. *Very* careful. Don't worry. What are you doing today?"

"I've got a day at home, remember?" Tessa replied. "It's a study day – preparation for exams! Though how I'm going to concentrate when I'm wondering all the time what Mrs Croker is up to, I don't know. I just wish we could go to her hide-out earlier, rather than later."

"Yeah, well, we can't," Roddy said. "And don't you risk it by yourself."

"I won't. You needn't worry!" Tessa said.

"We should be able to go tonight when we get back," Roddy whispered.

"OK."

Roddy strolled towards the bus in the school car park with William walking beside him.

"Are you coming on this trip or not, Roddy?" Mr Witt called.

"Sorry, Mr Witt," Roddy said. He hurried towards the bus and got on.

"Come on, Wally Crabbe!" Mr Witt shouted as Wally sauntered across the playground. "Chillwood Castle has waited six centuries to meet you. It can't wait any longer!" He gave an amused little smile. But Wally didn't think it was funny. He slouched on to the bus and sat down.

"Right," Mr Witt said as he stood at the front of the bus. "I think that's everyone." He closed the door. "Now, I'm afraid Mrs Justin won't be with us today after all, so..."

Just then the door opened and a panting, red-faced Old Nosey grappled his way up the steps.

"Pooh," he moaned. "Don't wait, will you?"

Everyone started laughing, except Wally.

"Omm, very sorry, Mr Harding," Mr Witt cried. "I thought you were already here."

"I've given up a day an' all for this. Fine thing, nearly settin' off without me!"

"Er. Yes. Indeed," Mr Witt said. "*Very* good of you, Mr Harding. Grateful beyond measure, of course. To step into the breach and help out at such short notice."

Loud groans and moans were heard and a solitary cheer from Wally.

"Omm, yes. That will do, I think. Now settle down and we'll set off on a nice, well-behaved journey."

He nodded to the driver. The driver had tattoos all over his arms and thick, greasy hair. Suddenly he slammed on a tape which blasted out heavy metal music. Then he revved up the bus as if it were a motorbike and roared out through the school gates.

Soon the ancient bus was rolling along the country roads towards Chillwood. Mr Witt sat next to Old Nosey.

"It does rock about, don't it?" Old Nosey said.

"Ugh," Mr Witt said. "I'm feeling ill already."

"Are you, Mr Witt?"

Mr Witt was turning pale, rolling his eyes about and rubbing his stomach.

"It reminds me of one time when I was on a boat, it do. I was with this bloke I knew. And he was like you, Mr Witt. He couldn't stand all this swaying and shaking about."

"Really?" Mr Witt managed to say.

"Not a bit." Old Nosey swayed around as if to demonstrate.

"Oh please! Mr Harding, don't!" Mr Witt begged. But Old Nosey was enjoying it.

"Oh, yeah. This bloke, we was on this trip and one day we'd had a whoppin' great bellyful of liver and onions. Yeah. We 'ad a plateful the size of a dustbin lid, we did, and this bloke, he starts scoffing them down like a big wallowing pig."

Old Nosey grinned and looked sideways at Mr Witt who had now turned grey.

"But then with the rolling and swaying of the boat he went green as a cucumber. Really green. And then he just puked up all over the deck, he did. We was steppin' and slidin' on bits of chewed up liver and onions. Up to our ankles in it, we was. Yeah. And I think there was a bit of egg in there an' all."

At this last remark, Mr Witt nearly threw up himself. Fortunately, the bus lurched into the car park of Chillwood Castle and came to a stop. Mr Witt leapt at the door, tore it open and ran to nearby bushes to be sick.

The children stared from the windows of the bus

at the gloomy bulk of the massive stone building which stood on a grassy earth mound.

"That looks really spooky," Wally Crabbe said, munching disgustingly through his last sandwich. He spat crumbs all over his neighbours as he spoke.

Old Nosey leered at the children.

"It's haunted!" he sneered, pointing his finger at the castle. "Well and truly haunted!"

The children watched the caretaker silently.

"Oh yeah," the caretaker went on nastily, "a few people have gone missing at this place. Even in broad daylight. Missing without trace! Might 'appen to some of you lot, if we're lucky. Eh?"

"Er, hum," Mr Witt said, looking extremely pale. He had poked his head momentarily through the open doorway.

"Oh, er, sorry, Mr Witt," the caretaker said with a smirk, "just trying to give the little 'orrors a taste of what this place is really like! I mean, for instance, did you know that on those walls up there, they reckon a ghost walks to her death every night and you can hear her screams all over..."

"That will do, Mr Harding!" Mr Witt called. "Let them get off the bus!"

Old Nosey sneered and slouched from the bus.

The children followed, straggling down the steps to gather in groups in the car park.

Mr Witt examined the notes on his clip board.

"Mr Harding," Mr Witt said, "if you'd take charge of group one, please..."

"Oh no!" Roddy groaned. "Just our luck to get Old Nosey!"

"Right then! Let's be 'avin you!" the caretaker shouted. "Follow me!" He strode off towards the castle like a sergeant major.

"Blimey," William whispered to Roddy, "he finks he's on parade at a barracks, don't he?"

The worksheets they'd been given were all carefully marked out so that even an idiot could follow them.

"Right, this is the first stop," Old Nosey bellowed. "Oi, you! Belt up, or else!"

"I wasn't talking," Amanda Bates replied.

"You listen to me," Old Nosey said. "I'm in charge here. So just shut that 'orrible little cake 'ole!"

He glared round the group.

"This is the gate-house. Read what it sez in your notes and no larkin' about. Notice the 'orrible spikes on the end of the gate. Them spikes had a purpose! What happened was, when anybody the soldiers didn't like was coming in to the castle, they used to drop them spikes down on them. Whoomff! And they'd squelch a man in two if he was daft enough to get caught under them." He gave a blood-curdling laugh.

"Brilliant!" Wally shouted.

"Huh. I don't think so," Amanda said.

"Hey, Roddy," Wally Crabbe said, poking his pencil through his worksheet and making a big hole in it. "Oops. What's this mean?"

"Portcullis?" Roddy said. "It's that criss-cross thing that Mr Harding has just been on about."

"What's it do, eh?" he said.

"It slides down inside those stone runners," Roddy said, "and shuts off the way into the castle."

"Yeah, right!" Wally Crabbe said. He wrote a sentence on his worksheet and wandered away to pester somebody else.

"Next stop!" Old Nosey yelled a few moments later.

"Oh, I haven't finished yet, Mr Harding," said Amanda.

"Never mind! You'll have to catch up later, won't you, you little morons?"

"Yeah, that's what they are, Uncle Jake!" Wally Crabbe laughed and pointed his finger at his group.

The rest of the children and Mr Witt followed more slowly.

"Ha ha," the caretaker laughed, "we're beating them lot! Come on, 'urry up you lazy little slouchers!"

"He's turning it into a race," Roddy said.

"It *is* a race, ain't it, Uncle Jake?" Wally said.

Old Nosey leered at him. "Yeah, course it is, Wal. Course!"

"He's got no idea," William muttered. "Blimey, he's just like some of my old customers on the boot stall. They was always carping on about me not being quick enough!"

As they crossed the interior court of the castle, the sun dipped behind a cloud and the whole lot turned greyer and colder. Old Nosey led the group inside the castle to a long room with a pit set in one corner. Over the pit was a grille. The children gathered round, peering down into it. A wicked little gleam came into Old Nosey's eyes. He lowered his voice.

"And what d'you reckon it was used for, eh?"

"Getting water?" Amanda said disdainfully. "It's a well, isn't it?"

"Ah!" Old Nosey tapped the side of his big hooter, "that's what you *would* think. But see that pokey little room over there?"

He pointed to a cell set into a wall. "People what couldn't be'ave themselves were locked in there. And then they'd chuck rotting carcasses down into this pit. Animals that had been dead for weeks."

"What for, Uncle Jake?" Wally said.

"Well, the stench and 'orrible stink, the gases and vapours and all that what came off of the rotting animals would come leaking out into this place and eventually kill the prisoners over that cell there. And I dare say that when the prisoners had snuffed it, they used to chuck them down the 'ole an' all. Now of a night-time, they reckon you can 'ear the 'owls of the dead coming up out of that 'orrible pit!"

"How cruel!" Amanda said.

The children gawped nervously through the grille.

"There's one down there," Old Nosey said, "called the Stickler, and he don't want naughty nitwits who drop litter around!"

"They didn't have litter years ago!" Amanda piped up.

Old Nosey's face went rigid, like a dishcloth left out in a frost.

"How old are you, squirt?" he said.

"Nearly twelve," Amanda said boldly, but her legs shook like jelly.

"Well, you listen to me, you shrunken little nerd. Litter has always been a problem ... even when the Stickler was alive!"

"Everything all right?" Mr Witt said, as he came striding towards Old Nosey's group.

"Yeah, course it is, Mr Witt," the caretaker said. "We're 'avin' a lovely time. Everything's just 'unky-dory, ain't it kids? I've just been telling 'em about the well."

"Oh good ... good!" Mr Witt said. "Without water, of course, a seige would soon be over. Omm, so it was, if you like, a vital part of any fortification."

"Anyway, must get on!" Old Nosey said cheerfully. "Can't get behind, eh, Mr Witt?" Then he marched away leaving Mr Witt looking uncomfortable.

Later in the afternoon, Mr Witt gathered everyone into a big group on a grassy bank inside the castle's walls.

"I think this would be a *splendid* place for a little sit down."

" 'Ere," William said. "Why's Old Nosey always scarin' people?"

"I don't know," Roddy said. "He gets some kind of strange pleasure out of it, doesn't he?"

"Yeah, well, I ain't gonna listen to him all afternoon. I'm gonna go an explore a bit."

"No!" Roddy said loudly.

"Not talking to yourself again, Oliver, are you?" Wally Crabbe sneered. "You're bonkers, you are."

"Oh, it was a huge wasp I saw on your head, Wally," Roddy said. "I thought it was going to sting you."

"Eh?" Wally shrieked. "Where is it? Has it gone?"

"Yes," Roddy said. He looked back at William. But William had also gone!

"Oh no!" Roddy moaned.

"Now what?" Wally said. "What's up?"

"Er, I forgot my bar of chocolate!" Roddy said.

"Huh," Wally scoffed. "You wanna be careful, Oliver, you might forget where you put your brain."

"Like you?" Roddy muttered.

"What did you say?" Wally growled.

"I said, *I like you*," Roddy lied. And then under his breath, "About as much as a dog's bottom."

Wally smiled awkwardly and then his face contorted into a sort of snarl. He didn't know what Roddy meant. But he had a vague idea that it wasn't what he thought it was.

Roddy got up and moved towards the entrance to the dungeons. Mr Witt didn't say anything, so Roddy nipped through the archway and down the many steps. It immediately became colder and gloomy.

"William!" he hissed. "William, where are you?"

Chapter 13

Dungeons

William *had* gone into the dungeons. But as he made his way towards what had once been the torture chamber, he heard the rattling of chains.

"What's that, then?" he said. He looked all around him, but couldn't see anything. When he heard the rattle again, he realized it was coming from the other side of a solid wall. "Right," he said. "Let's go and take a look." And he walked straight through a metre of thick rock and found himself inside a tiny cell. There was a strange old man inside it. He was in chains.

"Hello. You're a little bit early," the man said.

"Blimey," William replied. "You're a ghost! Ain't you?"

"I am now," the ghost of the old man said. "Eric's my name, and what be yours, young un?"

"William. William Povey, at your service, mate. Blimey! This is marvellous. I ain't seen another ghost for decades!" He stared at Eric and his eyes glowed brightly.

"You're early," Eric repeated.

"Early?" William said.

"For the Annual Ghost Meeting," Eric said.

"Annual Ghost Meeting?" William gasped.

"Oh, yes. And it's special. Lots of ghosts will be here on the solstice. Lots and lots of ghosts from all over the place. Special time, you see."

"Special?" William said.

"The hundred years are up," Eric said. "Every hundred years is very, very special. Haven't you come for that, then, young un?"

"Er. I dunno," William said. "I come 'ere with a school trip, but I'd like to come to the Meeting. Oh, I would."

"Then come you shall!" Eric said.

Suddenly they heard a voice calling.

"William! William!"

Eric looked at William.

"It's only me old mate, Roddy. Hang on, Eric, I'll just go an' see what he wants."

William appeared right in front of Roddy.

"Oh, there you are!" Roddy said. "I wish you wouldn't..."

"Come and meet somebody," William said. " 'Ere, 'old this." He gave Roddy a brush and led him through the thick stone wall. Both of them appeared in Eric's tiny little cell.

" 'Ere, you're not a ghost ... not a proper ghost ... are you?" Eric cried.

"No, I'm Roddy Oliver. I'm ... I'm here with my school," Roddy stuttered. "I ... I ... this is my time."

Eric stared at Roddy thinking about this.

"Your time? Your time? Ah, well, you are lucky to be alive!" he chuckled. "Eh, William?"

William laughed.

"Lucky to be alive, young un," Eric went on. "Now you take a word of advice from me who was alive in 1550 and dead ever since. You enjoy your life and make the most of it. Coz you're a long time dead."

William chuckled again.

"What?" Roddy said. "You've been down here in this place all that time?"

"I was, at first. They did wall me in here. The king's soldiers did it. They tortured me for stealing the king's deer. And then they put me in this little cell and fastened the door way up with stone and left me to die."

"That's horrible!" Roddy said.

"Aye. But I tell you, Roddy. I have scared a few folk since then. Quite a few! Including some of them that killed me."

"Pity you can't scare Old Nosey!" Roddy said.

"Old who?"

"He's a right bully!" William said. "He's with the school and he takes a real delight in scaring the kids half to death, he does."

"Oh," Eric said. "Well, you just listen here, Roddy. I can help." His chains became mysteriously unfastened from the wall. He dragged them round and clanked them noisily. Then he said, "You go and fetch Mr Nose down here! Go on, now! Fetch him quick!"

Roddy came running from the dungeons. "Mr Harding!" he called.

Mr Harding was standing in the middle of the

castle green. "Oliver? Not you again, you gormless little brat. What is it? Eh?"

"I've just been down the dungeons and there's something down there I bet would scare even you!"

"Get off, hokum pokum. What are you on about, you little blob of dripping? Eh?"

"It's down in the torture chamber. Really scary, Mr Harding! I bet you won't want to go down there, now, will you?"

"Who wouldn't?" Old Nosey leered. "What d'you take me for? Eh? I'm no wimp. Not like you! Just wait here you lot while I go and investigate what this twit has found. Huh!" he said. "I bet it's nowt. Nowt. Nowt at all!"

Old Nosey strode off down into the dungeons and very soon reached the torture chamber and went inside.

"What's that little toe-nail on about?" he chuckled as he looked around the room. There was hardly anything in it – just a couple of swords fixed to the wall and a couple of primitive instruments of torture.

"Ha! ha! ha!" he laughed. "Is that all that rat-tailed litter-twitter was on about?" He looked round the room. It was gloomy and damp. Not a comfortable place at all. Old Nosey turned to leave. As he did so, the door suddenly slammed shut.

"Eh?" the caretaker barked. He hurried to the door and tried to yank it open. But it was locked.

"Hey! Oliver, you dried up little piece of toadstool, come and let me out! NOW!"

Silence.

Old Nosey shook the door. "You just wait!" he seethed.

Then he heard the rattling of chains.

Eric had passed through the wall from his cell to the torture chamber. Old Nosey was startled.

"Who's doin' that?" he said angrily. "Hey? Is it one of you little stinkers?"

The chain rattled close to his ear. Old Nosey's jaw dropped. He looked frantically around the room, shocked to find himself feeling distinctly afraid.

"Who's there? Who is it?" he said, trying to control his voice. "If that's you flippin' morons, I'll ... I'll..."

Rattle, rattle, rattle.

"I ain't listening!" Old Nosey cried. He put his hands to his ears. But that didn't help.

Suddenly he gaped in terror. The two swords

fastened to the wall just in front of him lifted miraculously into the air. No hand held them. They seemed simply to draw from their resting places and swish angrily through the dim room. Whoosh! Swish!

Almost at once the swords clashed into each other as if they were fighting. They swirled and crashed round Old Nosey's head, sometimes splintering into the walls. When that happened the wall and swords gave off a shimmering spray of sparks.

"Oh my lord! It really is haunted!" Old Nosey whispered. "Oh, lord! Help!"

One of the swords suddenly stopped swinging and hung horizontally in the air before Old Nosey. The sharp blade pointed right at him. The caretaker stared at the point of the sword. He trembled from head to foot. Sweat broke out on his brow and dripped off his massive nose.

"Please..." he whimpered. "Please..."

The sword cut through the air in the room one last time and then joined the other one back on the wall. The door to the cell opened.

Old Nosey scrambled towards it. He tore along the dark corridor and up the dingy steps with the chains rattling at his heels. "I gotta get out," he shrieked. "I gotta get out!"

He raced out into the castle's grounds, gulping for air.

Roddy hurried back into the dungeons. "That was brilliant!" he shouted. "He was scared stiff! Thanks, Eric!"

"Mr Nosey might learn a lesson, eh?" said the ghost.

"Yeah," Roddy said. "He might!"

"Eric's been telling me all about a big meetin' here tonight," William said.

"Meeting?" Roddy replied. "What sort of meeting?"

"A ghost meeting. D'you wanna come?"

Roddy looked at William. He didn't actually fancy meeting a load of ghosts at all.

"Indeed, you are welcome to come to the AGM. And bring your sister as well!"

"I'll ask her," Roddy said.

"All right. Enjoyed meeting you, Roddy. Well met!" Eric said.

"Yeah," Roddy said. "You, too, Eric. And thank you."

When Eric had gone back to his cell, William

said. "Listen, Roddy me old mate, I was finkin', I may as well stay 'ere at the castle a little bit..."

"Stay?" Roddy said. "What d'you mean?"

"I ... well, mate, I got a lot to talk about with Eric. I ain't seen another ghost for donkey's years. I'll be all right. I mean, it's like you being with kids at school that you know."

"Yeah? OK," Roddy said.

"Here, you take these two brushes," William said. "Put them in your bag. And then you and Tessa could fly back here, couldn't you?"

"OK," Roddy said. "If she wants to. Otherwise..."

Suddenly Mr Witt's voice could be heard, shouting for everybody to get on the bus.

"I've gotta go," Roddy said.

William pushed the two brushes into his bag. "It's all right, mate. Blimey, don't worry. Just come back when you're ready."

Roddy nodded.

"What about ... you know?"

"The Ghost 'Unter? Don't worry about it. I'm safer here, anyway, ain't I? With other ghosts?"

"Roddy Oliver!" Mr Witt's voice called.

"But William," Roddy struggled, "what if we

find something out ... you know ... something important in the next day or two?"

"Do me a favour, then, mate," William said. "If you find out what she's up to, fly back and tell me!"

Roddy nodded. "See you then," he said.

"Yeah, see you, mate," William said.

Roddy turned and ran out of the dungeons and across the castle grounds to the car park. The bus was already being revved up by the driver.

"Come on, Roddy!" Mr Witt shouted. "Where on earth have you been, boy?"

Roddy scrambled on to the bus and moved down the aisle. As he did so, he noticed Old Nosey, sitting by himself, looking very pale.

Mr Witt sat at the front of the bus, away from the caretaker. He'd had enough of him on the journey there. He nodded to the driver who turned up the music and roared out of the drive as if he'd been kicked up the bottom by an elephant.

Suddenly, Wally Crabbe came down the bus to stand by his uncle. From behind his back he drew out a long plastic, replica sword – similar to the ones which had tormented Old Nosey in the dungeons. He held the point against his uncle's chest.

The effect on Mr Harding was electrifying. He jumped up with a start. His mouth dropped open. He went whiter than chalk. Then he let out a fearsome shriek.

"Get away! Get away!" he screamed.

"But it's only a souvenir, Uncle Jake!" Wally said. "What I bought from the shop!"

"What d'you want to go scaring folk for?" Old Nosey yelled.

"But I wasn't Uncle. I didn't mean to..."

Old Nosey dropped back into his seat. Wally shrugged and returned to his own.

Roddy couldn't stop thinking about William at Chillwood and about Eric and the AGM. He wondered if William really would be all right there. He didn't want to lose his friend. Not after all the fun they'd had.

The bus reached a T-junction. Roddy gazed vacantly out of the window. As he did so, he saw a white van. A very familiar, battered white van. Roddy leapt to his feet and stared hard at it as the bus pulled away from the junction. He swizzled his head round and craned his neck to see who was driving the van.

It was De-Sniff.

And sitting next to him – Mrs Croker. She was holding something in the air. It looked to Roddy like some sort of clock!

Chapter 14

Annual Ghost Meeting

"How was it, Roddy?" Mrs Oliver asked as soon as he got home.

"Oh ... er, fine," he replied. "Is Tessa in?"

"Aren't you going to tell us anything about Chillwood Castle?" his mother asked.

"Er ... yeah. It was great, Mum. Where's Tessa?"

"In her room. Your dinner's warming in the kitchen."

"Oh, OK," Roddy said. "I'll take it upstairs. I've got a lot to do ... notes and all that."

"Notes?" Mr Oliver laughed. "You're getting keen, aren't you, Roddy?"

Roddy ignored this, went into the kitchen, grabbed his meal and tore up to Tessa's room.

They both began speaking at the same time.

"Me first," Tessa bossed. "I'm the eldest! Where's William?"

"He stayed at the castle," Roddy replied.

"At the castle?" Tessa gasped. "But, Roddy, you surely didn't let him!"

"He wouldn't come! Listen, Tessa. We met another ghost!"

"What?"

"Another ghost. Called Eric. He and William got on like a house on fire. He just *wouldn't* come back with me."

Tessa noticed a look of sadness cross Roddy's face.

"But listen, Tess," Roddy went on, "I saw Croker and De-Sniff in their van. It was as we were coming home on the bus. They were going in the opposite direction. They were NEAR to Chillwood! They must have packed up their things, you know, after we'd escaped. It must have scared them. And they must have decided to head straight to Chillwood. So she *must* know about the AGM. She absolutely must!"

"AGM?" Tessa said.

"It's a big ghost gathering. Tonight!"

"So that's what the Ghost Hunter was on about!" Tessa said.

Roddy nodded. "And in the van she was holding something up ... it looked like a weird sort of clock!"

"That's the *Ghost Detecting Compass*!" Tessa cried. "It's leading her to the castle!"

"We've got to do something!" Roddy shouted. "There's going to be loads of ghosts there and I'm sure the Ghost Hunter is on her way to bottle the lot. And William!"

"What time does it start?" Tessa said.

"Midnight," Roddy said.

"Midnight?" Tessa groaned. "We can't do anything, then, can we? We can't get there in time!"

"Look what I've got!" He showed Tessa the two shoe-brushes lying at the bottom of his school bag.

"Brilliant!" Tessa squealed. "Roddy, you're incredible!"

"Yeah," said Roddy. "I know!"

"Those two are as thick as thieves," Mrs Oliver said later to her husband. "Roddy has hardly shown his face since he came in."

"And there hasn't been one row!" Mr Oliver added. "Maybe they're just getting on. It does happen."

"I don't know. I've just got that feeling they're up to something."

"Well, why don't you look in on them before we go to bed?" Mr Oliver said.

"Yes, I think I will, dear," Mrs Oliver said. "I'm going up now. My researches have quite exhausted me today! There's all sorts of energy around the village at the moment, but it seems to be missing me out!"

Mrs Oliver went upstairs quietly and peeped in on Tessa. The room was in darkness and Tessa was curled up under her duvet. Mrs Oliver looked in Roddy's room.

"Goodnight," she whispered.

But Roddy didn't reply. He, too, was tucked up, fast asleep. Mrs Oliver closed the door gently, smiled to herself and gave a sigh of relief.

If she'd looked closer, she would have found pillows stuffed under the quilts, topped by an old wig in Roddy's bed, and the long hair of an old doll in Tessa's.

The two bird-like children flew rapidly under a moon-lit sky towards Chillwood Castle. The wind whispered through Roddy and Tessa's hair.

Beneath them, pale trees, roofs, roads went by. Soon they reached the outlying wood which wound itself around the Chillwood Estate like a huge collar. The castle itself looked gigantic and romantic, encircled by its ancient moat. Its water glistened in the pale light of the moon.

"There's no sign of the van!" Tessa cried.

"No," Roddy said. "But they weren't coming in this direction for nothing, I bet."

The pair of them circled the castle and came down over the battlements and alongside the vast main structure.

"In here," Roddy said, pointing to a massive stone wall.

Tessa nodded and they passed straight through the wall and found themselves standing in the Great Hall.

"Wow!" Tessa whispered, and her voice echoed round the room. They stood for some moments in the middle of the immense room. It was as quiet as the grave. Suits of armour glistened in the soft moonlight which came in through huge high windows.

Some candles were burning in holders.

Almost immediately, Roddy and Tessa heard a

terrible, ghastly moaning and into the Great Hall came a floating knight, dressed in chain-mail. As he moved slowly forwards, dragging himself on stumbling ghostly legs, Tessa gave a gasp and clasped her hands to her mouth. The knight had a sword sticking out of his back. Blood stained his armour. His face was as white as parchment.

He groaned again as he dragged himself past them.

Now through another door, came the ghost of a tightrope walker. She balanced on a ghostly wire, doing stunts up in the air. She twirled and twisted, turned somersaults and handstands and finally fell to the ground in a horrible way – as if she was repeating an accident which had happened to her in a circus or travelling troupe many years ago.

As she fell, Tessa turned to Roddy. "Awful!" she whispered.

Even as she spoke, another ghost floated forwards – a beautiful lady dressed in a tall wimple and long grey gown. Her face was grey, her hair was grey, her hands were grey. She looked imperiously at them as she passed.

"We-ird!" Roddy muttered fearfully.

"Good grief!" Tessa squirmed. "Just look at him! Look at his head!"

Roddy blinked and rubbed his eyes.

Coming towards them with a slow, regular pace was a ghost dressed in a blood-stained tunic. Above his white ruff was nothing. Instead, all they could see was his neck poking up out of his collar. But under his arm he was carrying a hairy bundle with two eyes peering from it.

Then the bloodless lips began to speak.

"This won't hurt a bit! Off with his head! This won't hurt a bit!"

Many other ghosts swarmed into the Hall and formed a circle right round Roddy and Tessa.

"Let's get out of here!" Roddy hissed. "I don't like it!"

"Where's William?" Tessa said.

"I don't know," Roddy said. He stared at the ghosts. "They look so ... *scary*!"

The ghosts wavered all around them, floating up and down in a misty haze. Roddy had just made up his mind to leave when William arrived. Roddy and Tessa hurried to him.

"Oh, William!" Tessa cried out. "It's terrifying!"

William looked at them.

"Hello," he said. "So you came after all?"

"We ... we..." Tessa was mumbling and staring at the ghosts.

"Don't be scared, me old chums," William said. "They're all really friendly."

"They don't look it," Roddy whispered.

"You'll soon get used to them. You was scared of me, remember? An' I ain't done you no 'arm, 'ave I?"

Roddy and Tessa fidgeted. But they were very glad to see William.

"This is Eric," William said.

"Pleasure to meet you," Eric said to Tessa. "And you again, Roddy, me lad!"

"Cor blimey," William shouted, "I never knew there were so many flippin' ghosts about!" He smiled at Tessa and Roddy. "All right?" he said. "You've come for the AGM?"

"No," Tessa hissed, anxiously. "We've got bad news."

Eric heard her and came forward.

"Bad news?" he said.

"The Ghost Hunter," Roddy said. "Mrs Croker. I saw her and De-Sniff, coming this way, when I was on the bus going home. I'm sure it was them!"

William turned even paler than he already was.

"The Ghost 'Unter? Here?"

"I don't know if she's *actually* here. But she was coming this way," Roddy said.

Just as Roddy was speaking, a very superior-looking ghost wafted up to them in long strides. His piercing eyes stared at Roddy and Tessa.

"What are you doing here?" he demanded.

"Oh, Lord Chillwood," Eric said. "I'd like to introduce..."

"I said, *what* are they doing here?" he pointed a spectral, quivering finger at Roddy and Tessa. "They're *not* ghosts, are they? They have no right to be here at all!"

"It was me, Lord Chillwood," Eric said. "My doing."

"How have they done this?" he growled. "Become like ghosts?"

"I lent them me brushes," William said. "Blimey, it ain't a crime, is it?"

"It's a big mistake," Lord Chillwood said, coldly. "Nobody should do this!" he glared at William.

"They came to warn us!" William said. "An' you oughta listen to them."

"What d'you mean? Warn us?" Lord Chillwood snapped. "What can harm us?"

"The Ghost Hunter!" Roddy said. "She's on her..."

"Ghost Hunter!" Lord Chillwood sneered. "What ridiculous nonsense! There's no such thing. It's just a bogeyman, made up to frighten child ghosts, to make them behave!" He seized the brushes from Roddy and Tessa. "And I'll take these, so they won't be misused any further!"

Roddy and Tessa became solid at once.

"Now leave!" boomed Lord Chillwood.

"But ... but ... she's here!" Roddy tried again. "She wants to bottle..."

"There's nobody here!" Lord Chillwood hissed. "Nobody that shouldn't be, except you two! If there was, I'd know about it! D'you think I don't know what's going on right under my own nose? Now, will you leave at once!"

Roddy and Tessa turned helplessly to William and Eric.

"But that ain't fair, sir," William cried. "They can't get back 'ome without them brushes."

"They shouldn't be meddling in ghostly business!" Lord Chillwood said. "Now get out! Or

I'll have you thrown out."

"We're going!" Roddy snapped. "And if the Ghost Hunter gets you, that's your hard luck!"

"Steady on, Roddy," Eric said. "Steady."

Roddy and Tessa walked out of the huge hall and hurried down the stairs. Tessa was crying.

Lord Chillwood marched away, still carrying William's shoe-brushes.

William turned to Eric.

"They're my friends, Eric! They saved me bacon! And they're not talkin' rot when they say the Ghost 'Unter is out there! I know, mate. I seen her before! She's real! She was after me!"

"Lord Chillwood, he don't listen to folk at all," Eric said.

"I've got to go after them," William said. "I can't just let them leave like that!"

"You're quite right, Will," Eric said. "There's a little bit of time yet before the midnight stroke which is when we must be at the AGM. I shall come along with you."

"That Lord Chillwood'll be sorry when he gets shrunk and stuck in a bottle," Tessa said angrily as she and Roddy walked along one of the long

132

corridors of the castle trying to find their way out.

"Yeah," Roddy replied. "Where d'you reckon old Croker and De-Sniff are, anyway?"

"I don't know," Tessa cried. "Perhaps they weren't coming to the castle at all."

"Wrong!" a horrible voice screeched.

Out of the darkness swooped a huge, black shape, like a massive bird of prey. Roddy and Tessa fell back against the wall, holding their arms up to their faces as Mrs Croker threw herself at them, knocking them to the ground. Tessa screamed as De-Sniff grabbed her. Roddy tried to roll away, kicking out and punching. But the great cloak fell round him, swamping his flying feet and fists.

"You stupid little weasel!" Mrs Croker's voice hissed as she clawed at him, trying to hold him.

"Get off me!" Roddy yelled, struggling. He tried to get back on his feet, but he couldn't. The Ghost Hunter spat and cursed. Then she got his right arm in an iron grip and twisted it up his back.

"Ow!" Roddy yelled in pain. "Ow!"

De-Sniff was still grappling with Tessa.

"Get off me!" she shrieked. Tessa kicked and struggled for all she was worth, but De-Sniff was surprisingly strong despite his skinny frame.

"Get out of that, scum-bag!" he snarled, as he pinned her down.

The children were thrown into a small room. The door was locked and bolted. "Got 'em!" De-Sniff crowed. "They won't be no more trouble now, boss."

"Quiet!" Mrs Croker snapped. "Someone else is coming!" Her nose started trembling. Her eyes went misty and far away. "I smell ghost!"

Roddy and Tessa banged on the door and shouted, but the room was off the main corridor and their voices were muffled by the thick walls.

Mrs Croker rammed De-Sniff into a dark recess and pressed herself beside him. Mrs Croker's breath came fast. De-Sniff was so excited, he nearly choked trying to stop himself from snuffling. Eric and William came round the corner of the corridor. Mrs Croker's nose twitched frantically. She could barely hold herself back as the ghost smell grew stronger and stronger. Eric and William got nearer and nearer. Nearer and nearer.

Mrs Croker wrenched the Ghost Immobilizing Vapour Gun out of a deep pocket in her cloak and muttered to herself, "No escape this time, ghost boy! No escape at all!"

Chapter 15

The Midnight Hour

"They can't have gone far!" William said as they came down the corridor.

"No," Eric said. "Unless they ran quicker than we think."

"I wonder if they're in there," William said. "Roddy! Tessa!" he called out gently as he ducked into a small closet.

Eric walked on a few steps and then waited for him.

"Take that!" Mrs Croker screamed as she sprang out of the dark corner she had been hiding in and sprayed Eric at close range with GIV.

De-Sniff gave a whoop of glee as Eric became completely visible. He could no longer move. His face contorted into a mask of horror and pain. But it was no use. In an instant he shrank to the size of a small doll. There were tears in his eyes. Tears which had begun to roll down his old crinkled cheeks.

"Bottle him, you idiot!" Mrs Croker barked when she saw De-Sniff standing gawping at Eric.

"Yes, boss!" De-Sniff yelled. He grabbed Eric by his hair and shoved him roughly into a bottle which he took out of a bag they'd brought with them.

"Now, where is that other one?" Mrs Croker sniffed. She could still smell William. He was hiding round the corner, aghast at what had happened to Eric. He trembled violently. Mrs Croker swooped round the corner towards him howling, "Take that, you ghost trash!" She sprayed wildly. But the spray gun was already empty. Nothing more came out of it.

"The gun!" Mrs Croker cried. She turned on De-Sniff in a fury. "It's run out!"

"Weren't my fault, boss. I filled her up to the brim, I did! You been using it too much!"

Mrs Croker let out a terrible cry of anger and hurled the spray gun at De-Sniff.

William now vanished through the ceiling. He felt heart-broken about his friend. But for now there was nothing he could do.

"You gormless half-wit!" Mrs Croker screamed at De-Sniff. "Why didn't you do something? Instead of standing there like some half-baked, brain-dead mawkin?"

"It weren't my fault the vapour ran out, boss!" De-Sniff whimpered.

"That's your job! You're the assistant! You should have made sure there was a replacement! Useless! We'll have to go to the van for a refill!"

She stormed away in front of De-Sniff, calling over her shoulder, "Come on, hurry up! There's more here. Lots more! And I'm going to get the beasts. D'you hear me? Get them all!"

"Yeah, boss. Right, boss," De-Sniff called. "And I got a big 'un in the van an' all. A really big 'un!"

Roddy and Tessa continued yelling from their cell.

"It's no use," Tessa groaned at last. "Nobody can hear us down here. Nobody at all."

"Oh yes, they can!" William said. He drifted down in front of them from the direction of the ceiling.

"William!" Roddy and Tessa shouted together.

"Thank the saints I've found you!" William cried. "That fiend has got Eric!"

"Where is she?" Roddy said. "Is she still out there?"

"No," William said. "I fink they've moved on. Come on, we gotta be quick!" He passed through the massive oak and undid the bolt. Roddy and Tessa hurried out into the gloomy corridor.

"We must get back to the Great Hall," Tessa said. "Before Croker and De-Sniff do!"

"And you'll just have to make that Lord Chillwood listen to reason," Roddy cried. "Tell him about Eric!"

A wild expression passed over William's face at the mention of Eric.

"If that old fool 'ad listened! Pompous old pig!" he cried. "Eric would still be 'ere!" Ghostly tears appeared on William's cheeks, flowed down to the floor and vanished.

The three children cautiously made their way back to the Great Hall. When they reached the main door, William said, "You'd better wait 'ere. If Lord Muck sees you, he'll 'ave a fit!"

"We'll watch out for Croker and De-Sniff," Roddy said. "And if we can, we'll try and stop them. But let's just open the Great Door a crack so that we can keep our eye on what happens to you in there."

Tessa gently eased the door open so that they could peep into the crowded room. "Listen, Roddy," she said, "I'll go and see if I can find out where De-Sniff has parked the van. I mean, if I could find it, I might be able to get rid of their GIV supply,"

"It's not safe," Roddy said.

"I know it's not safe," Tessa hissed, "but it's not safe being here, is it?"

"All right," Roddy said. "But come back as soon as you can!"

Tessa patted his arm and moved quickly and quietly away.

Roddy watched the Great Hall again. He saw William gliding swiftly forwards through a crowd of ghosts of every kind. They were all facing Lord Chillwood, who hovered in the air at the front above everyone.

"This is the Great Meeting," Lord Chillwood said grandly. "Only once in a hundred years does this event take place, when we ghosts are allowed to be as we once were – for a few fleeting moments."

A murmur of interest spread through the crowd of ghosts.

"Some of you have come a long way to be here at

this special place at this special hour." Lord Chillwood turned and looked towards a great clock as the finger moved slowly towards midnight. "I welcome you all."

"Sir!" William shouted. "The Ghost 'Unter's here!"

All heads turned as William drew near to Lord Chillwood.

"What is the meaning of this?" Lord Chillwood growled.

"She's here, in the castle!" William shouted.

A strange ghastly whisper rustled and rippled through the crowd.

"Not again!" Lord Chillwood bellowed angrily. His eyes flared with blue burning lights. He gestured to two strong-looking ghosts across the room.

"Throw this ragamuffin out! I've never heard such piffle in all me life! Pah! Ghost Hunters indeed!"

"It's true!" William shouted. "Listen everybody. There is a Ghost 'Unter in the castle and she is very dangerous and if we don't do something now..."

"Be quiet!" Lord Chillwood thundered. He

nodded to the two bouncers who flew at William, and shoved him through the doors.

"She's caught Eric! She's already bottled him!" he yelled.

But at that moment, the clock struck twelve. To everyone's delight, the ghosts all took on solid form once again.

A hum of joy and pleasure replaced the rumble of fear which William's talk of the Ghost Hunter had created.

"You've got to listen to me!" William yelled to the two bouncers, but they rushed back into the hall in high spirits.

"Blimey," William said, "I feel funny. I feel just like a new boy, I do."

Roddy stared at William's pink hands and William felt his own skin and hair.

He grinned.

"You *look* like a new boy!" Roddy said.

All the ghosts were talking at once in a great hubbub when the door to the high minstrels' gallery burst open and on to it rushed Mrs Croker and De-Sniff.

"Good grief!" Mrs Croker whispered. "They're all ... I can see the lot of them. They've all materialized! Just look at the revolting beasts! Look at the repulsive, monstrous freaks! Where do they all come from!"

"I can see em an' all, boss. What's gone wrong?" De-Sniff said. He was shivering with fear.

"Wrong? Nothing's wrong, you idiot! It's the solstice, isn't it? The special one! That's why all these hideous creatures are here! Unnatural fiends! Ghouls and creatures! They will remain like this for only a short time, and if even so much as a drop of my Ghost Immobilizing Vapour touches them, they'll be done for sooner or later! Agh! I'm going to bottle the lot of them!" she screamed madly. All eyes swung towards her. She was glaring down on them like a demon. And in her hands she clutched, not a small pistol, but a huge industrial spray nozzle which could spurt Ghost Immobilizing Vapour everywhere.

"Pump, De-Sniff! Pump!"

De-Sniff began pumping. Pumping and sniffing. Sniffing and pumping. As the handle of the pump went down and up, so lashings of snot splashed from De-Sniff's nose on to the floor.

"Pressure's building, boss!" De-Sniff managed to cough. He was sweating and his eyes were popping with terror as they turned to stare at the ghosts.

The ghosts were flummoxed. They twisted round and round wondering what to do.

"Get out!" William shouted from the doorway. "It's Ghost Immobilizing Vapour. A drop of it on you will shrink you. Get away! Get away!"

Suddenly a great spouting arc of the stuff shot up into the air. The ghosts screamed in alarm and rushed towards the door.

"More pressure, De-Sniff! More pressure!" Mrs Croker howled as she turned the hose, this way and that, trying desperately to hit a ghost.

A great dash of GIV skimmed past Lord Chillwood's ear. He dived away, realizing now that the danger he had so stupidly refused to believe in was right at the heart of the castle. Another splurge of GIV ploughed past the grey lady and splatted against the suit of armour behind her.

"More pressure!" Mrs Croker screamed. Her face was aflame with hatred and excitement. "We've got the lot of them here!"

The ghosts were in a blind panic, bumping into each other and creating a scene of chaos in the

Great Hall. Roddy knew he'd got to do something quickly.

"You stay there, William!" he called. "Keep out of the way!"

Roddy darted to the staircase which led up to the gallery. He bounded up the steps, threw open the door and barged into De-Sniff with all his might. De-Sniff, half-exhausted by his efforts on the pump, fell over. The spray dried to a dribble. Roddy rushed at Mrs Croker. He snatched the nozzle from her hands and threw it on the floor.

Mrs Croker was livid with anger. Her eyes narrowed to two fierce black points of light. She clawed at Roddy, but De-Sniff, who was himself struggling and kicking to get up off the floor, tripped her up. The Ghost Hunter went sprawling in a puddle of drippings from the hose.

Roddy grabbed the pipe which was connected to the pump and yanked it free. Then he hurled it over the gallery's rail so that it crashed to the floor of the Great Hall below.

Mrs Croker spat menacingly as she clambered to her feet again. "You meddler! You twerp! You festering, interfering idiot! I'll tie you in knots! I'll chew you up in pieces and spit you down the drain! I'll..."

But Roddy dashed for the door. De-Sniff tried to stop him, but his dive missed and he went sprawling into the pump, banging his head and nearly knocking himself out. Through the door and up the stairs to the tower, Roddy ran. Anywhere! Just to get away from her.

"After him!" Mrs Croker shrieked. "I want him dead or alive. Preferably dead!" She roared through the door and was just in time to see Roddy dash under the arch which led to the stone stairway up to the tower.

Chapter 16

The Tower

Tessa had followed the corridor of the castle until it led to a door to the outside. When she opened it she realized there was a narrow path leading round to an old out-house. Much to her delight, she found the van hidden in one of the buildings. She approached it cautiously and when she realized there was nobody in it, she opened the rear doors. To her amazement she saw hundreds of bottled ghosts – many of the ones she'd seen before at the hide-out. She gasped, putting her hand across her mouth.

"Oh, heavens!" she cried. She looked round for something to break the bottles with, and then wondered if it might do even more harm.

It might even finish them off altogether, she thought.

She closed the doors quietly – there was no GIV left that she could see. Then she made her way back to the driver's door. She thought perhaps there might be some GIV under the driver's seat. Before she reached it, however, a great banging came from inside the van.

To her amazement, the van began to glow with a deep pink and yellow light. It became strangely soft, as if it wasn't made from steel at all. It looked more like the petals of a lovely flower, caught in the rays of a bright sun. Quite unexpectedly, through the sides of this phantasm, slid semi-transparent figures.

Tessa stared in astonishment. There were men and women, boys and girls. And as they passed out of the van, they assumed a solid human form. More and more of them poured out of the van and began walking away, with bouncing steps. They were laughing and joyful. Tessa heard the castle clock sound the last stroke of twelve.

"Midnight," she whispered. "It must be the solstice that's caused it."

Eric was the last person to leave the van. Tessa and he watched it return to its white metal state. Mrs Croker's bottles lay in the back of the van, smashed to pieces by the ghosts' transformation.

"I never thought I'd see the world again," Eric cried. He wiped away a tear.

Tessa looked at him.

"All those ghosts she'd bottled," she murmured. "All free now!"

"Where is the Ghost Hunter?" Eric asked. "Is she still here?"

Tessa came to her senses, as she realized that the crowd freed from the van was heading straight for the castle.

"Wait," she shouted. "Don't go up there!"

But none of them would listen to her – they didn't even seem to hear her, so happy and excited were they to be free.

As Tessa chased after them, to try to head them off, Eric followed more slowly. He was still in a daze. His head was fuzzy, his eyesight a bit clouded. He decided to sit down on the grass for a few minutes, until he felt better. Tessa and the other ghosts went out of sight. Suddenly Eric saw a thin figure running away from the castle. He didn't realize at first that it was De-Sniff. But when he did realize, he could see that the Ghost Hunter's assistant was in a panic, and was obviously trying to get away.

Eric's head began to clear. He began to feel the power of the blood coursing through his veins, and felt the muscles which had been unused for centuries spring back into action.

"Ho!" he said, stepping out from behind a bush right in front of De-Sniff. De-Sniff stopped, rigid with fear. His eyes flickered, nervous and shifty.

"Get out of my way ... old m-man," he stuttered.

"In a hurry, Ghost-Hunter Apprentice?" Eric boomed. He raised his gnarled fists ready to fight. De-Sniff shifted from one foot to another.

"I ain't doing any harm. Just clearing off, that's all!"

Eric danced closer, enjoying his new-found vitality.

"Not doing any harm, eh?" he said. He landed a punch on De-Sniff's nose. "Well, that's for the harm you've done already!"

De-Sniff staggered and Eric gave him a chance to get back on his feet.

"Let's see what you're made of," Eric said, "without the old battle-axe behind you!"

De-Sniff snarled and hurled himself at Eric.

They fell and rolled over and over, tussling on the grass. Eric soon got the better of him.

"Not so handy on your own, are you?" Eric cried. But as he spoke, he felt a tingling which started in his toes and travelled upwards through his whole body.

"Oh, no," he groaned, as he started to fade back into his phantom body.

"Oh, yes!" cried De-Sniff, in triumph. "Oh, yes, you ghost twit. No escape this time!"

He pulled out of his grubby pocket a small GIV sprayer. Before Eric had completely vanished, De-sniff let him have it, full in the face.

Nobody else heard Eric's cries as he was frozen, shrunk and bottled once more. And this time, there would be no solstice to bring him back. De-Sniff threw him into the van and drove off as fast as he could go.

Roddy ran quickly up to the top of the highest tower in Chillwood Castle. He emerged on to the roof under a sky laden with silver stars and a shining moon. He ran to the parapet and looked over the edge. A long, long way below, the moat shone darkly.

Mrs Croker gasped and panted her way to the top of the steps until at last she, too, came out on top of the roof.

"He's here, De-Sniff!" She looked round for her apprentice. "De-Sniff?"

Roddy twisted around.

"Got you anyway," Mrs Croker crowed, her face turning a strange purple colour and her eyes a fierce, burning red. "There's only one way down from here – for you, you interfering little pest." She paused for a moment, getting her breath back. Then she began creeping stealthily, dangerously, towards him.

"I've had more than any normal person can stand!" she hissed.

"Only you're not *normal*, are you?" Roddy said. "You're odd. Very odd!"

"You're the one that's odd, you hopeless boy. Liking ghosts! Nothing normal in that. Worse than vermin!"

"They're nice," Roddy said. "I'd rather spend a day with a ghost than one minute with you!"

Mrs Croker bared her teeth. Roddy drew back in fear.

"Ghost adorer," she whispered. "Ghost keeper. Ghost lover!"

She drew back the sleeves on her huge cavernous cape and her long fingers arched into a pair of nasty-looking claws with fingernails like hooks. "Ghost saver. Ghost saver. Deserves to have an accident!"

"If you think you'll get away with anything," Roddy said nervously, "you'd better take a look behind you."

"What?" she snapped. "Oh. Behind me. That old trick. I don't think so."

But she did glance quickly over her shoulder anyway. And as soon as she did so, she let out a terrible cry. William, Lord Chillwood, the grey lady and many many more ghosts floated there. Some of them were very angry.

"You bottled us for years!" one shouted.

"You're a demon!" another screamed.

Mrs Croker twisted round to face them. She had her back to Roddy now and seemed to have forgotten he was there as she jumped up on to the high parapet of the tower.

"You vermin!" she shrieked. "How have you got free?"

The ghostly crowd came closer, closer, closer. Some of them reached out to her with pale fingers, but Mrs Croker darted across the stones of the ledge she was standing on.

"How?" she screamed. "You were all bottled! And you'll all be bottled again. You should be bottled. *For ever!*"

The ghosts seethed and hissed at her. As they got closer, she grew more and more demented.

"Where's De-Sniff?" she shouted. "De-Sniff! Bring the vapour! I'll do for them now!"

Suddenly, as she waved her arms frantically about in the air, her foot slipped on the damp stone. The Ghost Hunter wobbled and circled her arms to keep her balance. Her mouth contorted, her lips darkened to purple. She scrambled and struggled to save herself as her tall body was snagged by the wind. Her face screwed up into a horrible mask. And then she fell.

She toppled backwards and plunged from the lofty parapet down to the moat, fifty metres below. She hit the water with an almighty SPLASH!

Roddy and Tessa rushed to look. But the surface of the moat had already closed over her and seemed as smooth and still as a millpond. The water shimmered faintly in the pale moonlight.

Roddy stared round him in a state of shock.

"There's no sign of her!" he cried.

"It's all right now," Tessa said. "It's over. She's gone!"

"Bottomless," whispered the grey lady, peering over the parapet.

William patted Roddy's back. "You've done a wonderment, Roddy me old mate. A wonderment you 'ave done!"

The rest of the ghosts cheered. Most had already reverted to their flimsy ghostly state and floated and drifted about in the cool night air.

Lord Chillwood came forward. He stood in front of Roddy, Tessa and William with his head bowed.

"I was an arrogant old fool. Can you ever forgive me?" he said, handing the shoe-brushes back to William.

Roddy looked up and smiled. Lord Chillwood shook his hand.

"Blimey, mate, we all make mistakes, don't we?" William said chirpily. Then he started looking round him. "Where's Eric? I can't see 'im."

Roddy scanned the crowd of ghosts with his friend. He shook his head. "Nor can I. And what happened to De-Sniff?"

William stared at him. There was a look of panic

now in his eyes. "He's gone, ain't he? That crafty little creep!"

He called round to the other ghosts to see if any had seen him. They hadn't.

"I heard an engine a few minutes ago," Roddy said. "You don't think he's..."

"Look, Roddy!" William said urgently. "I gotta get after him. Eric ain't here ... and if De-Sniff has got him, you know what, don't you?"

"He'll have bottled him," Roddy said.

"Take these," William said. He thrust the two shoe-brushes at Roddy and Tessa. "Just in case, eh?"

Then he smiled tensely at them.

"It's been great. And we beat that old Croker, didn't we?"

"But, William," Roddy said. "You're not going off on your own?"

"I got to. I got to save Eric!"

"But you will keep in touch with us, won't you?"

"I will if I can," William said. "I really will." He was already rising into the air. "You better get off home yerselves. I gotta go now. Before De-Sniff gets too far in front of me."

"Bye," Tessa said.

"Yeah. Bye, me old mates."

"Bye," Roddy said. "See you soon?"

But William was already flying swiftly away over the castle walls.

Chapter 17

The Last Threads

At school a few days later, Mrs Justin was back. "Are you better now, Miss?" Amanda Bates asked her.

"I feel completely well now, thank you!" she beamed at them.

"It's because there weren't no ghosts after all, miss," Wally Crabbe suggested. "Only Uncle Jake havin' a bit of a joke!"

"Well, it didn't feel like a joke at the time!"

Mrs Justin looked round smugly at the very tidy room.

"Mr Harding seems to be doing a much better job these days, doesn't he?"

"So he ought," Roddy muttered.

"He's a brilliant caretaker!" Wally called.

A few of the children groaned at this.

"Right," Mrs Justin said. "No more talk about silly ghosts. We all know now that they simply don't exist, don't we?"

Roddy smiled and thought sadly of William. He missed him very much already and wondered if he'd found De-Sniff yet.

"By the way," Mrs Justin said. "Mr Witt thought you'd like to know – as you have recently been to Chillwood Castle – that the moat has recently been drained. Somebody claimed they had seen a person fall into it from the tower the other night. Mr Witt told me to tell you that the moat is actually a very early one and very deep. He thought you'd be interested in that."

Roddy sat up. "Was there, miss?" he said.

"Was there what, Roddy?"

"A body, miss. In the moat?"

"No," Mrs Justin said. "The moat was completely empty. It was all a false alarm. They found nothing at all except a big, old black cloak. And now, I believe, it's time to do some more science, isn't it?"